CHRISTOPH

THE CASE OF THE AMATEUR ACTOR

CHRISTOPHER BUSH was born Charlie Christmas Bush in Norfolk in 1885. His father was a farm labourer and his mother a milliner. In the early years of his childhood he lived with his aunt and uncle in London before returning to Norfolk aged seven, later winning a scholarship to Thetford Grammar School.

As an adult, Bush worked as a schoolmaster for 27 years, pausing only to fight in World War One, until retiring aged 46 in 1931 to be a full-time novelist. His first novel featuring the eccentric Ludovic Travers was published in 1926, and was followed by 62 additional Travers mysteries. These are all to be republished by Dean Street Press.

Christopher Bush fought again in World War Two, and was elected a member of the prestigious Detection Club. He died in 1973.

CHRISTOPHER BUSH

THE CASE OF THE AMATEUR ACTOR

With an introduction
by Curtis Evans

DEAN STREET PRESS

INTRODUCTION

Ring out the Old, Ring in the New
Christopher Bush and Mystery Fiction in the Fifties

"Mr. Bush has an urbane and intelligent way of dealing with mystery which makes his work much more attractive than the stampeding sensationalism of some of his rivals."
—Rupert Crofts-Cooke (acclaimed author of the Leo Bruce detective novels)

New fashions in mystery fiction were decidedly afoot in the 1950s, as authors increasingly turned to sensationalistic tales of international espionage, hard-boiled sex and violence, and psychological suspense. Yet there indubitably remained, seemingly imperishable and eternal, what Anthony Boucher, dean of American mystery reviewers, dubbed the "conventional type of British detective story." This more modestly decorous but still intriguing and enticing mystery fare was most famously and lucratively embodied by Crime Queen Agatha Christie, who rang in the new decade and her Golden Jubilee as a published author with the classic detective novel that was promoted as her fiftieth mystery: *A Murder Is Announced* (although this was in fact a misleading claim, as this tally also included her short story collections). Also representing the traditional British detective story during the 1950s were such crime fiction stalwarts (all of them Christie contemporaries and, like the Queen of Crime, longtime members of the Detection Club) as Edith Caroline Rivett (E.C.R Lorac and Carol Carnac), E.R. Punshon, Cecil John Charles Street (John Rhode and Miles Burton) and Christopher Bush. Punshon and Rivett passed away in the Fifties, pens still brandished in their hands, if you will, but Street and Bush, apparently indefatigable, kept at crime throughout the decade, typically publishing in both the United Kingdom and the United States two books a year (Street with both of his pseudonyms).

Not to be outdone even by Agatha Christie, Bush would celebrate his own Golden Jubilee with his fiftieth mystery, *The Case of the Russian Cross*, in 1957—and this was done, in contrast with Christie, without his publishers having to resort to any creative accounting. *Cross* is the fiftieth Christopher Bush Ludovic Travers detective novel reprinted by Dean Street Press in this, the Spring of 2020, the hundredth anniversary of the dawning of the Golden Age of detective fiction, following, in this latest installment, *The Case of the Counterfeit Colonel* (1952), *The Case of the Burnt Bohemian* (1953), *The Case of The Silken Petticoat* (1953), *The Case of the Red Brunette* (1954), *The Case of the Three Lost Letters* (1954), *The Case of the Benevolent Bookie* (1955), *The Case of the Amateur Actor* (1955), *The Case of the Extra Man* (1956) and *The Case of the Flowery Corpse* (1956).

Not surprisingly, given its being the occasion of Christopher Bush's Golden Jubilee, *The Case of the Russian Cross* met with a favorable reception from reviewers, who found the author's wry dedication especially ingratiating: "The author, having discovered that this is his fiftieth novel of detection, dedicates it in sheer astonishment to HIMSELF." Writing as Francis Iles, the name under which he reviewed crime fiction, Bush's Detection Club colleague Anthony Berkeley, himself one of the great Golden Age innovators in the genre, commented, "I share Mr. Bush's own surprise that *The Case of the Russian Cross* should be his fiftieth book; not so much at the fact itself as at the freshness both of plot and writing which is still as notable with fifty up as it was in in his opening overs. There must be many readers who still enjoy a straightforward, honest-to-goodness puzzle, and here it is." The late crime writer Anthony Lejeune, who would be admitted to the Detection Club in 1963, for his part cheered, "Hats off to Christopher Bush....[L]ike his detective, [he] is unostentatious but always absolutely reliable." Alan Hunter, who recently had published his first George Gently mystery and at the time was being lauded as the "British Simenon," offered similarly praiseful words, pronouncing of *The*

Case of the Russian Cross that Bush's sleuth Ludovic Travers "continues to be a wholly satisfying creation, the characters are intriguing and the plot full of virility. . . . the only trace of long-service lies in the maturity of the treatment."

The high praise for Bush's fiftieth detective novel only confirmed (if resoundingly) what had become clear from reviews of earlier novels from the decade: that in Britain Christopher Bush, who had turned sixty-five in 1950, had become a Grand Old Man of Mystery, an Elder Statesman of Murder. Bush's *The Case of the Three Lost Letters*, for example, was praised by Anthony Berkeley as "a model detective story on classical lines: an original central idea, with a complicated plot to clothe it, plenty of sound, straightforward detection by a mellowed Ludovic Travers and never a word that is not strictly relevant to the story"; while reviewer "Christopher Pym" (English journalist and author Cyril Rotenberg) found the same novel a "beautifully quiet, close-knit problem in deduction very fairly presented and impeccably solved." Berkeley also highly praised Bush's *The Case of the Burnt Bohemian*, pronouncing it "yet another sound piece of work . . . in that, alas!, almost extinct genre, the real detective story, with Ludovic Travers in his very best form."

In the United States Bush was especially praised in smaller newspapers across the country, where, one suspects, traditional detection most strongly still held sway. "Bush is one of the soundest of the English craftsmen in this field," declared Ben B. Johnston, an editor at the *Richmond Times Dispatch*, in his review of *The Case of the Burnt Bohemian*, while Lucy Templeton, doyenne of the *Knoxville Sentinel* (the first female staffer at that Tennessee newspaper, Templeton, a freshly minted graduate of the University of Tennessee, had been hired as a proofreader back in 1904), enthusiastically avowed, in her review of *The Case of the Flowery Corpse*, that the novel was "the best mystery novel I have read in the last six months." Bush "has always told a good story with interesting backgrounds and rich characterization," she added admiringly. Another southern reviewer, one "M." of the *Montgomery Advertiser*, deemed *The Case of the Amateur Actor* "another Travers mystery to delight the most critical of a reader audience," concluding in inimitable American lingo, "it's a swell story." Even Anthony Boucher, who in the Fifties hardly could be termed an unalloyed admirer of conventional British detection, from his prestigious post at the *New York Times Books Review* afforded words of praise to a number of Christopher Bush mysteries from the decade, including the cases of the *Benevolent Bookie* ("a provocative puzzle"), the *Amateur Actor* ("solid detective interest"), the *Flowery Corpse* ("many small ingenuities of detection") and, but naturally, the *Russian Cross* ("a pretty puzzle"). In his own self-effacing fashion, it seems that Ludovic Travers had entered the pantheon of Great Detectives, as another American commentator suggested in a review of Bush's *The Case of The Silken Petticoat*:

> Although Ludovic Travers does not possess the esoteric learning of Van Dine's Philo Vance, the rough and ready punch of Mickey Spillane's Mike Hammer, the Parisian [sic!] touch of Agatha Christie's Hercule Poirot, the appetite and orchids of Rex Stout's Nero Wolfe, the suave coolness of The Falcon or the eerie laugh and invisibility of The Shadow, he does have good qualities— especially the ability to note and interpret clues and a dogged persistence in remembering and following up an episode he could not understand. These paid off in his solution of *The Case of The Silken Petticoat*.

In some ways Christopher Bush, his traditionalism notwithstanding, attempted with his Fifties Ludovic Travers mysteries to keep up with the tenor of rapidly changing times. As owner of the controlling interest in the Broad Street Detective Agency, Ludovic Travers increasingly comes to resemble an American private investigator rather than the gentleman amateur detective he had been in the 1930s; and the novels in which he appears reflect some of the jaded cynicism of post-World War Two American hard-boiled crime fiction. *The Case of the Red Brunette*, one of my favorite examples from this batch of Bushes, looks at civic corruption in provincial England in a case concerning a town counsellor who dies in an apparent "badger game" or "honey trap" gone fatally wrong ("a web of mystery skillfully spun" noted Pat McDermott of Iowa's *Quad City Times*), while in *The Case of the Three Lost Letters*, Travers finds himself having to explain to his phlegmatic wife Bernice the pink lipstick strains on his collar (incurred strictly in the line of duty, of course). Travers also pays homage to the popular, genre altering Inspector Maigret novels of Georges Simenon in *The Case of Red Brunette*, when he decides that he will "try to get a feel of the city [of Mainford]: make a Maigret-like tour and achieve some kind of background. . . ."

Christopher Bush finally decided that Travers could manage entirely without his longtime partner in crime solving, the wily and calculatingly avuncular Chief Superintendent George Wharton, whom at times Travers, in the tradition of American hard-boiled crime fiction, appears positively to dislike. "I generally admire and respect Wharton, but there are times when he annoys me almost beyond measure," Travers confides in *The Case of the Amateur Actor*. "There are even moments, as when he assumes that cheap and leering superiority, when I can suddenly hate him." George Wharton appropriately makes his final, brief appearance in the Bush oeuvre in *The Case of the Russian Cross*, where Travers allows that despite their differences, the "Old General" is "the man who'd become in most ways my oldest friend."

"Ring out the old, ring in the new" may have been the motto of many when it came to mid-century mystery fiction, but as another saying goes, what once was old eventually becomes sparklingly new again. The truth of the latter adage is proven by this shining new set of Christopher Bush reissues. "Just like old crimes," vintage mystery fans may sigh contentedly, as once again they peruse the pages of a Bush, pursuing murderous malefactors in the ever pleasant company of Ludovic Travers, all the while armed with the happy knowledge that a butcher's dozen of thirteen of Travers' investigations yet remains to be reissued.

Curtis Evans

PART I

The Case of Gordon Posfort

1

ONE DEAD MAN

I suppose my life has been no more cluttered up with coincidence than that of any other man: in fact I have to think pretty hard to recall anything of the kind that would be even worth the telling. But that evening—the 10th of November, 1953—I did happen to be thinking of George Wharton and wishing that something might turn up in the murder line, with myself called in as a stooge to George—or, more politely, as what the Yard calls an unofficial expert.

I wish no harm, mind you, to my fellow men, and all I wanted was a kind of academic murder: no blood and all problem. Or perhaps the murder might be that of someone who really ought by universal consent to have been murdered long ago, so that even finding the murderer would be academic too. Or perhaps the whole thing was that I was too much at a loose end and wanted something interesting to occupy my days. Bernice—my wife—was away for at least a fortnight with a very aged but resilient aunt who was having yet another of her frequent relapses. Things were quiet at the Broad Street Detective Agency and Norris—the managing director—could easily cope with the present routine. In fact, before I had begun day-dreaming about a nice intricate murder, I had been almost tempted to think once more about that proposition that Gordon Posfort had made to me, even though I knew I should once more turn it down.

However, I went back to my crossword and pencilled in another clue or two. And it was then that the telephone went. I knew it couldn't be Bernice, for she had rung me just before that scratch meal which had taken the place of dinner.

"That you, Mr. Travers?"

"Yes," I said.

"This is Scotland Yard, sir. Hang on a minute, will you?"

I didn't think about murder, though I knew it would be George Wharton. I had seen him a couple of days before and we had talked vaguely about a dinner together and then a show.

"Hallo. That you, Travers?"

"In person, George."

"You're still not busy?"

"Far from it."

"Right," he said briskly. "Slip along, will you, to the Royalty Hotel, Room 323. A man's been shot there. Matthews thinks you might be able to identify him. I'll be along myself in a few minutes. Got it? Room 323."

For a moment I didn't know what to say, and then it was too late. I hung up the dead receiver and made for my overcoat and hat. Not that I really wanted either. You remember, perhaps, that extraordinary early winter weather, with its mugginess by day and its quite warm nights with merely a flicker of mist. And the Royalty was only about four minutes from the flat. I actually got there with a few seconds to spare, and it was exactly half-past seven when I went through the swing doors of that vast, conveyer-belt sort of caravanserai.

The hot air met me and there was the same old smell, almost fetid, of too many people and too much heating, and with it an odour of meals and tobacco and furniture polish. People were milling everywhere—at the long reception desk and the kiosks, and there were queues at the lifts. I took the stairs two at a time, and with my long legs I didn't have to give the semblance of a jump. At the last landing the indicator board told me that Room 323 was to the left, so I went along a corridor and then had to turn left again. This time the corridor was short and at the end angle a man was standing, neck craning cautiously round.

I wondered what he was peering at. My feet made no sound on the thick carpet, so I gave a cough as I neared him and he whipped round at once. Then he shot away and ahead of me to the left. I had to turn to the right, and it was all so quick that I didn't get too good a sight of him, even in profile. I did notice that he had very fair hair, a nose slightly hooked, and that he was about five feet nine and probably in the late twenties. As for that Peeping Tom business, I knew almost at once what and why it was, for only half a dozen doors along was Room 323. He must have come by it from the other way and seen something happening: a glimpse of Matthews and a plain-clothes man or two, perhaps, through the suddenly opened door. Maybe he had even got a glimpse of the corpse.

I tapped at the door and went straight in. Matthews gave me a grin. He and I had worked together—suffered under Wharton, shall we say?—long before he had even dreamed of becoming an inspector. Old Doc. Anders gave his dry smile and nod. Matthews introduced me to the third man, Warren, the hotel manager.

"Wharton rang me about identifying a body," I said, and my eyes went beyond the single bed to a sort of hump that lay on the floor, just short of the dressing-table and covered with a blanket. That would be the corpse, and it was only then, curiously enough, that I was really wondering why it should be I who was likely to identify it.

"Here we are," the doc. said cheerfully. "Have a good look at him."

Corpses, to the professionals, are just something in the day's work. I'm more squeamish, especially where there's blood: but then, as I've said before, I was never cut out for a professional sleuth. Maybe Anders saw something of that in my wary approach.

"Not a messy job. Just a few bullets pumped through his navel."

There was a grunt from Matthews and I turned away. There was no mess: just a dark stain one could see on the waistcoat. What was horrible was the contortion of the face and the tortured eyes. But even then I thought I knew him. Anders stooped and turned the head from profile to full front.

"Recognise him?"

"Yes," I said, and my fingers were suddenly at my glasses. "He's a man named Gordon Posfort. A literary agent."

There was a grunt from Matthews and I turned away. What Posfort should be doing in that hotel I couldn't imagine. The

Royalty was the sort of place he'd have said, ironically enough, that he'd hate to be found dead in.

"A bit of a shock to you?" Matthews said. "I mean, he was a friend of yours?"

"No," I said. "Not a friend. He belonged to the same club as myself and we'd had some talk about business from time to time. As a matter of fact I saw him on business only last week. But why did you think of me to identify him?"

Doc. Anders passed me his cigarette-case.

"The whole thing's queer," Matthews said. "We were absolutely up a gum-tree about who he was till we found that little engagement book in a fob pocket. It had your name in it."

It was a little red book, lying on the side table with oddments that had been taken from the pockets.

"My name," I said. "Would it be an entry for last Thursday? For eleven o'clock? That was when I last saw him."

He flicked the pages over with his gloved fingers.

"That's it, sir. What about these other names for the same day? Know any of them?"

I knew none personally and only one, a writer of historical novels, by repute.

"All you can assume is that they're clients of his," I said. "You can test it in the morning. The office—Drench and Posfort, the name is—is at 229 Brent Street, Strand."

Then I remembered something else.

"What's this about everything being queer? You mean you found no papers on him that might have identified him?"

"There's far more than that," he said. "Look at him. Overcoat on and his hat just beyond him. His head towards us. After what you've just told us, this is what must have happened. He came here to see what you've called a client. We think two men were waiting for him. One shoved a gun in his waistcoat and backed him towards that window, then he let him have the lot, clean through the belly. One of them went quickly through his pockets while the other peeped out of the door. They took his wallet and papers and were in such a hurry that they missed that book.

Then they walked out, leaving that fibre case in the corner there. All it's got in it are half a dozen bricks wrapped in newspapers."

There was nothing I could say. Queer wasn't the word for it.

"Mind you," Matthews was going on, "we don't think all that without some outside evidence."

He broke off to cock an ear. I heard a familiar cough in the corridor and in came George Wharton.

It didn't take me long to know that George must have had a pretty full report from Matthews. He gave a quick look round, nodded generally and let an enquiring look linger on Warren. Matthews introduced him. Over George's face came an expression that was a subtle mixture of the official and the condoling.

"A bad business, this, Mr. Warren. Still, we'll try to make as little trouble as possible. You co-operate with us and we'll do the same with you."

Then he whipped round on me.

"You could identify him?"

Matthews told him all about it. Could you have seen the expressions on the face of George—Chief-Superintendent Wharton to you—you might have learned quite a lot about his deliberate eccentricities: the faint disapproval, for instance, that I should have known the man at all, and a certain gratification that one who had moved in the same social circles as myself should have met with an abrupt end. George professes to hate snobbery: he talks sneeringly about those whom he is apt to term my Oxford and Cambridge friends: he can allude as sneeringly to his own superiors as the Big Bugs, and yet I would call him the arch-snob of all my acquaintance.

But he did make a note or two in his book before he turned to Warren. Would the manager mind nipping downstairs and seeing if there was any more news about the registration of the room we were in.

"That's got rid of him," he told us when the door had closed. "Tell me about those timings again, Matthews."

"About seventeen minutes past seven were the shots," Matthews said. "The chambermaid was in the linen room about two doors up and she heard what she called a series of quick knocks. She was getting an extra pillow for a man just recovering from influenza in 325, just across the corridor, and he'd turned off a wireless programme at seven fifteen and he heard the noises just after that and he and the chambermaid checked up when she brought the pillow in. She had a look in the rooms and came to this one. The man was just dying, apparently, and she claims to have heard his last words."

"Clear enough," Wharton said. He pursed his lips in thought and the huge moustache stood above them like an awning. "Photographs taken?"

"Yes, sir."

"Prints?"

"Only a quick check. None whatever so far except the chambermaid's."

"Right. Let's have her in."

"What about getting him away?" Anders said. "Looks as if I'm going to have a pretty messy job, and I'd like to get on with it."

Wharton glared.

"What do they pay you for?" He turned to Matthews. "What's this chambermaid like?"

Matthews made a face.

"The usual. Pretty reliable, I'd say, sir. Warren spoke well of her. She's been here for five years. Name's Lumley. Ellen Lumley."

"Right," he said. "Get her here."

He pulled out his pipe, thought better of it, and fumbled in the breast pocket of his old blue overcoat for his spectacle case. He hooked on the antiquated glasses, and he did it as solemnly as if he didn't know that we both knew the whole thing was a fake. But they did change his looks. As that chambermaid came in, with his shoulders slightly stooped and a best bedside-manner smile hovering on his lips, he could have soothed a charging tiger.

"Miss Lumley—or is it Mrs.?"

"Miss . . . sir."

"I wouldn't have thought it," he told her. "Still, there's plenty of time."

She was a good witness, even if she did keep her eyes away from that blanket. I put her at about thirty-five: no beauty, admittedly, but with a frank if somewhat frightened face.

"Nothing to be worried about," Wharton was telling her soothingly. "You must have had a pretty bad shock, but I can see you're not the kind of woman to give way, as they say. So just take your time and tell us what happened. Begin at when you were getting that pillow."

Everything tallied with Matthews's version.

"And when you actually came in this room?" prompted Wharton.

"Well, sir, I'd knocked, as I said, and no-one answered, so I let myself in and there was the gentleman lying on the floor and I must have told myself he'd had a fit or something and that was the noises I heard. I mean, when he fell. He was sort of trying to support himself on one side and groaning and looking awful, so I asked him what was the matter."

She moistened her lips.

"I was all sort of . . . well, I just sort of did it. I didn't know what was the matter with him and I thought he might tell me. I thought he was trying to say something, so I bent down and asked him if he was ill, and that was when I heard him say what I told this gentleman here, about how they'd got him."

"Got him!"

"Yes, he said they'd got him."

He gave a grunt. Out went the moustache again as he pursed his lips.

"Look here, Ellen. You mustn't mind me calling you that. I'm old enough to be your father. I'd like you to do something for us. There's the man, as you see, underneath that blanket, and he's dead. We shan't take the blanket off, but we want you to imagine you're just coming into this room as you were when he was taken ill. You'll do that for us?"

She said, nervously, that she'd try. It took a good ten minutes before everything was over.

"That's it, then," Wharton told her. "I knew you could do it. So you had your ear practically against his mouth. Even then you could only just catch what he was trying to say, and no more. The words were: 'They got me', and then another 'They'."

"Yes. It was as if he was trying to say it again, and then he sort of fell over on his face and I thought I was going to faint."

"Ah! But you didn't," Wharton told her. "You're not the fainting kind. You rang down to the office. You kept your head. Mr. Warren was telling us how reliable you were, and now we know it. And that's about all we want, Ellen, thank you. We may have to get a statement from you later, but you needn't worry about that. It'll only be putting down in writing what you've just told us."

He went ahead to open the door for her, then halted.

"You like it here, Ellen?"

She gave a little smile.

"Well, yes, I suppose I do. Or I shouldn't have been here as long as I have."

There was a gratified nod.

"Give you plenty of time off, do they?"

"Well, I get what I'm entitled to."

"Yes," he said, and gave a wry smile. "That's about all any of us get nowadays. Fond of the cinema, are you?"

"Oh yes."

"Go often?"

"Not here. It's far too dear. I go with my sister, though. She lives at Hendon. You can get cheaper seats there. Ever so much cheaper."

"And who's your favourite film star? Gary Cooper?"

"Oh no." There was no nervousness now in the smile, and Wharton might have been a favourite uncle. "I think he used to be once. Now it's Alan Ladd. Him or John Wayne."

"Ah well, it's nice to be young." He moved on to the door. "Good luck to you, Ellen, and thank you again."

He watched for a moment from the open door, and when he turned back he was hooking off those glasses. He looked round at us and his lip curled.

"They got me!"

The words had an infinite scorn.

"What did she think we were? A pack of fools?"

I like George Wharton. I generally admire and respect him, but there are times when he annoys me almost beyond bearing. There are even moments, as when he assumes that cheap and leering superiority, when I can suddenly hate him.

"She was only a fool in one thing," I said.

"Oh?" He glared. "And what was that?"

"Because she didn't see what you were driving at over that cinema palaver."

The smile was still more of a leer.

"She wasn't meant to see it. Call yourself a detective?"

"I'm not," I said. "I'm plain Ludovic Travers: a private citizen who was asked to come here and identify a body. I've done it, so I'll say good night, George, and get along home."

"Now, now, now," he told me placatingly. "Why take me seriously? You know me better than that."

You'd have thought I'd done him some mortal hurt. I knew the whole thing was ersatz, but somehow I didn't go any nearer to the door.

"Look at the whole thing without any prejudice," he was telling me. "Mind you, I don't say she didn't hear something, but look at her state of mind, suddenly coming in here and seeing him here on the floor and so on. Everything, though she mightn't have known it, was pure cinema. Gangsters, rustlers, six-shooters. They got me, pal, and all that sort of thing."

I could have pointed out something if he'd have given me the time—that she had had no idea that he'd been shot. But he was going right on.

"This man Posfort. A literary gent, you said?"

"So to speak—yes."

"You think a man like that would have used that cinema language? *They got me?*" He shook his head. "Think what you like, but I can't swallow that."

"All the same, someone did shoot him."

"When you gents have finished," Anders broke in, "what about getting him away?"

Then Warren came in. He and Matthews went down with the stretcher men to a side door and the ambulance. That fibre case went with them for the Back-Room Boys to look over. Wharton, who had watched from the door till they were out of sight, came in again and began stoking his pipe.

"What exactly was that chap Posfort doing here?" he asked me almost casually.

I didn't answer for a moment. My brain's far more agile than his, though, in the long run, maybe, less reliable, so I'm generally pretty quick with a theory. The trouble is that if that theory proves to be wrong, then it stays as mine. If it happens still to look likely, then it's ours; if by any chance it happens to be a winner, then it's George's own.

"I thought I told you," I said. "He'd never have come to an ant-hill like this if it hadn't been to meet a client."

Then my fingers moved suddenly towards my glasses.

"Wait a minute, though. He wouldn't have come here to meet the sort of client who'd be staying in an hotel like this. He'd have fixed an appointment for his office."

"Might have been something else?"

"I'm beginning to think so. He must have been lured here for some reason that satisfied him." I shook my head. "Still, it might have been a client who claimed to be temporarily bed-ridden, like that chap across the corridor who's getting over flu. But I don't like it."

"What about a woman?"

"Could be," I said. "A woman might have fired those shots. And I happen to think he was just that kind of man."

"Yes," he said. "I think this is going to be a remarkably tricky business. Anything else strike you?"

"Only in the same context," I said. "Someone must have hated him mighty badly to have given him that kind of death."

The door opened for Matthews. Warren was with him, and he had got all he was likely to get about the registration of the room. It had been booked the previous day by telephone and it had been taken up the next morning just before noon. The receptionist had no idea what the man—his name had been given as Corland—had looked like. Noon was a busy time and there would be a long queue at the desk. Only when a client had a peculiar name or a peculiar look or had got into some muddle over his registration would a receptionist be likely to recall him. In any case, the fact remained that no-one did recall him.

"If it's any use to you, here's the actual registration form," Warren said.

We all had a good look at it under Wharton's glass. The name, as the regulations demanded, was printed in neat capitals, and was Humbert Corland. The place of origin was given as Belfast and the nationality as British.

"Mind if I keep this?" Wharton said.

A minute or two and Warren was leaving. I said I'd be going too.

"Why the hurry?" Wharton asked me. "It's only just nine o'clock. What about telling us all you happen to know about this chap Posfort?"

"Why not?" I said.

The room was stuffy with its central heating and I took off my overcoat and got out my pipe. George offered me the room's only chair, but I preferred the bed. What I told him and Matthews took perhaps no more than ten minutes. What I tell you would have taken far longer. Then I was talking and had little time for thought. Now I have that time and can emphasise and keep things logical, and there are some I can afford to omit. What I do assure you is that both versions have and had everything that was likely to prove relevant to the case of Gordon Posfort, the man whom I had seen for the last time, with six bullets in his belly and lying on a stretcher as they took him from Room 323.

2

BACK IN HARNESS

IT WAS in 1946, just after the war, that I first saw Gordon Posfort. I rarely trouble to look at the notice-board in the club to see what people are up for membership and it's only when I see someone new that I have any desire to know if the man is merely a guest or a new member.

I saw Posfort sitting alone in the reading-room after lunch one day and I asked the man who was with me who he was. He knew Posfort sufficiently well to introduce me, not that I wanted to go that far. However, we had a few words together and I learned that he was a literary agent and that the man who had put him up was Sellick-Browne, the historian. Later I looked him up in a reference book. He had been to one of the smaller public schools, and from there had gone straight to Hillock and Holt, the publishing firm. Matthew Holt was his uncle, and the idea had probably been that the young Posfort should work his way up through the departments and be groomed for something really important in the firm. At twenty-six he had married, his wife being a niece of Alfred Hillock. Three years later he had left the firm to join Drench and Clark, as it then was, the firm of literary agents.

It is women who are said to talk the scandal. Maybe they do, but men aren't altogether averse. Pick the right men at the right time and you can hear any club scandal in all its details. Not that it hadn't puzzled me why Posfort should have left his uncle's firm with its undoubted prospects, for, as you may possibly gather, I'm the most curious man alive. If there's something that puzzles me I just have to have an answer, and in Posfort's case I soon had the right one. It was that his wife had divorced him, and therefore it had most likely been Alfred Hillock who had got rid of him.

In that literary agency he found his milieu. He had had that experience of publishing and he was a go-getter. And he had the right manner, or manners: a sympathy and understanding that one only later might think a bit too suave, and a grasp of things and a flow of words that could convince and practically mesmerise. And he was remarkably good-looking: tall, easy-moving, sleek-haired and fine-featured, and with a voice both cultured and charming. He had too a quality of agelessness, for when I saw him on that 3rd of November he had looked almost the same as when I had first seen him eight years before in the club. The sleek black hair had never a hint of grey and the voice was merely the least bit more resonant.

Bernice didn't like him. He once did me a favour and I asked him to lunch, and it was after it that she told me he wasn't a nice sort of person. I was entirely in disagreement, even if I didn't actually say so, and even when her dislike of him turned out to have a not unusual reason—that he had looked at her as if she were naked. Bernice, I should say, even in her late thirties, is a remarkably good-looking woman. Then later I changed my mind about Posfort.

It was when he approached me after lunch one day at the club and asked me to have a port with him. Then we sat chatting and at last he mentioned a couple of books I'd written on crime matters a few years before and asked what they were doing. I said they were still selling in tiny driblets. Then he suggested handling them himself and outlined various things he could do with them. I said my original agents were still handling them.

"Oh, them!" he said. "Hopelessly out of date, my dear fellow. Notorious. Everyone knows they can't sell a thing."

That was why I didn't like him and that kind of go-getting, and once you've seen any sort of crack in a man's veneer, you soon begin to espy others. Mind you, I admit that once or twice I had to make a polite use of him when a particular case happened to need information about something connected with his profession. I also got to know later another member of the firm—Lilian Rome—a competent and delightful woman of about forty-five who handled certain of the firm's clients. I also was on smiling terms with a very charming secretary-receptionist whose name I didn't know.

But about that last visit of mine to Brent Street on the 3rd of November. I had a letter from Posfort asking me to see him about a proposition he would like to put up to me: something, he said, that would be both interesting and remunerative, and he suggested the date and time. I rang him in order to find out what the scheme was, but he refused to talk about it over the telephone, so I agreed to meet him.

I hadn't been to Brent Street for about a year, and when I went into the enquiry hall I saw a new secretary-receptionist: a sleek, good-looking blonde in the twenties. Seductive was hardly the word for the smile she gave me and she actually had one of those husky voices you read about but never somehow hear. She said she'd see if Mr. Posfort was free. The voice over the buzzer said apparently that I was a bit early and would I mind waiting just a minute or two. So I took a seat and the lady went on with her typing.

"There used to be a dark, quite good-looking girl here," I said. "Is she ill or has she gone?"

"You mean a Miss Halsing," she told me evenly. "She's been gone quite a time now. Almost three months."

"To get married?"

There was a slight droop of her lip.

"I'm afraid I don't know. But I don't think so. I think she turned out rather unsuitable."

I could have said that it had taken quite a long time to discover that, but then Lilian Rome happened to pop in.

"Hallo!" she said. "You waiting to see Gordon?"

"Yes," I said. "He should be ready for me in a minute or so."

"Come and wait in my room. I want someone to talk to. Tell him Mr. Travers is with me, will you, Miss Barnes?"

There had been a subtle change in her tone as she said those last words: a definite frigidity, and not, I thought, because she was giving instructions to a subordinate. However, I went through to her room and we began chatting about this and that. Then in one of those sudden gaps in conversation I mentioned that receptionist-secretary, Miss Halsing.

She frowned.

"Most tragic," she said. "Poor Caroline! Did you know about it?"

"Know about what?"

"Well, she suddenly left us and I could never gather why. She always seemed most happy here. A most charming girl and everyone liked her. She actually cried when I said goodbye to her and I couldn't get her to tell me why."

She gave a slow shake of the head.

"Then we heard the news, about a month or two ago. She'd committed suicide."

"Good God, no!" I'd just been seeing her in my mind's eye and it had been somehow more than a shock. "What was the reason?"

"We don't know," she said. "It was all rather hushed up. It might have been ill-health—"

The buzzer went then and almost at once she was showing me through to Posfort's room. Just short of it she said something rather strange.

"Don't mention anything of what we were talking about to Gordon. I think it upsets him."

What he and I talked about, or perhaps what I listened to, was that proposition of his. Briefly it was this. I had been engaged on very many famous murder cases, he said, and thanks to having given evidence on numerous occasions I was something of a public figure. That took care of what might be called the publicity side. As for the actual proposition, it was this. Some of the cases on which I had been engaged must have been unsolved. I was to give an account of such cases and suggest solutions in the light of afterthoughts or subsequent knowledge. It was as simple as that. Also he knew of a publisher who'd be delighted to take such a book or books, and an American one, and a French one who was practically a certainty.

I turned the whole thing down and he looked positively aghast.

"But there's money in it, my dear fellow! A whole lot of money. If it's a question of time, you could sketch things out and I could get it written up for you."

I mightn't have looked too annoyed, but I did tell him that if I ever published anything under my name, then it would be I who wrote it, even to the last full-stop.

"Sorry," I said, "but it's something I just don't care to do. Outside the question of getting the permission of the Yard, there's the fact that a good many people connected with such cases are still alive. Sorry again, but there it is."

That was how we left it, or so I thought. But he couldn't leave it like that and two days later I had another letter from him, taking my objections one by one and trying to skirt round them or demolish them. I rang him and told him somewhat forcibly that I still wasn't changing my mind.

But I was to see him again under very different circumstances. On the Monday afternoon Bernice had that letter from her aunt's companion and decided to go to Dorset. She sent a telegram giving the time of arrival and then set about packing. That was a longish business, since she didn't know for how long the visit might last. To ease things, or as a kind of palliative to parting, I suggested we might dine out and I booked a table at the Cap d'Argent in Shepherd's Street—one of the lesser-known restaurants where I'd always found the food remarkably good.

We had a table on the ground floor and it was when we were well into our meal that I saw Posfort having a confidential word with the head-waiter, who was motioning him upstairs. I had dined up there once with George Wharton, and it was a far more intimate place, with little booths arranged round one of the inner rooms. Not that all that was particularly important. What was important was that Posfort didn't see me though I saw him, and the woman who was with him. It was that blonde secretary, and when he moved to take the stairs in the outer hall, she took his arm and smiled up at him with a kind of adoring possession.

"And that's everything, George," I said. "That's about all I can tell you about Gordon Posfort. It's up to you to make use of it—if there's anything in it you *can* make use of."

George blew out that moustache of his, then lighted the cold pipe. Matthews cut in.

"I can't help thinking there must have been something fishy about that other girl's suicide. If it doesn't do anything else, it might give us a lead."

"Yes," Wharton said slowly. "There might be something in that. What sort of a girl was she?"

"I've told you," I said. "A brunette of about twenty-five: not actually a beauty but very attractive looking. Very nicely and intelligently spoken. Very well educated, I'd say, and charmingly mannered and poised. The sort of girl you'd like to be seen out with, and in any company."

"Then what was she doing in an office?" he fired at me.

I stared.

"Depends what you mean by office. She wasn't just a typist. In fact I think that you'd have been very happy, George, if your own daughter had had such a job. Interesting work and meeting interesting people and probably quite well paid."

"All right," he said. "You needn't bite my head off. The thing is, what do you think about it yourself? Was this Posfort carrying on with her? Was that why she left—because he'd got her into trouble or something? Was that why she committed suicide?"

"There may be something in it," I told him, "but aren't we rather rushing ahead? A whole lot of things have to be explored, as I see it, before we come to that."

"Such as?"

"Look, George," I said, "I came here, as I told you, as a perfectly ordinary citizen to identify a body and then to say what I knew about him. Where do I stand now? Am I having my few brains picked just for the fun of it? Am I working for the Yard or the Agency or just for me?"

"Who's rushing ahead now?"

"No-one," I said. "I just want to know where I stand."

"All right," he said. "Let's assume things turn out so that you're in on this case. Now what do you suggest?"

"Probably what you know yourself," I told him. "Everyone on this floor and the one above it will have to be questioned about seeing a man or men enter this room. That's a pretty big job. Side by side with it there'll have to be a microscopic probing into the life of Posfort. You can't even rule out the possibility that this job may have been done by someone whom he double-crossed in business, or even some disgruntled client."

He grunted.

"Well, you knew him and his office. You could take over that side of it. Have who you like with you. When will you begin?"

"As I see it," I said, "I ought to begin at once. There might be all sorts of covering of tracks. You give the word and I'll get to work straight away. It isn't too late."

"What about keeping in touch with you?"

"If you're going back to the Yard, then I'll see you there," I said. "It might take another hour or so, but I'll be there."

I went straight down to Warren's office, found Lilian Rome's address in the telephone directory and rang her. She was in.

"This is Travers, Ludovic Travers. I've got some rather urgent news for you which I'd sooner not mention over the telephone. I know it's rather late, but might I come along at once and have a quick word with you?"

"You sure it can't wait?"

"Nothing to do with business," I said. "But listen, Miss Rome. I'm not being flippant about this, but if you don't agree that the visit was justified I'll buy you the best hat in town."

I heard her give a little nervous laugh.

"If that's so I can't refuse. At once, you say?"

"In about a quarter of an hour."

The taxi made it dead on time. At the flats I didn't use the lift, but took the stairs to the second floor and Flat 27. As soon as I rapped on the door she opened it.

Out of her office she was quite an attractive woman. The rather severe garb had been changed to a blue frock that matched her eyes and she had given herself a different hair-do. I had guessed her age as forty-five, but it turned out to be over fifty. That night she looked well under forty.

"Come in," she said. "And what's all this important news?" She laughed. "You see how rude I am? Even before asking you to have a drink. What *will* you drink?"

"At the moment—nothing."

"Then let me take your hat and coat. You're looking very serious."

"Am I?" I smiled and dodged the question. The room was cosy and very warm and very feminine. The easy chair that I took was like one immense cushion.

"Now," she said, and took the chair opposite me and leaned towards me across its arm. "What *is* this terribly important news?"

"Gordon Posfort's dead."

She stared. For a moment she was utterly still, then her tongue slowly moistened her lips.

"An accident?"

"No," I said bluntly. "He was murdered. In a room at the Royalty Hotel."

"Oh, my God!"

I wondered why her face had not paled but had flushed so violently red. I looked away from her and at the electric fire.

"I was called in to identify him," I said. "Now I'm taking part in the official enquiry. You'll have to take my word for that."

She was getting to her feet. At the side table she poured herself a drink and squirted a little soda. I heard the gulp as she drank, and the glass, as she came back to the chair, was still half full.

"It's been a shock," she said. She looked away, then her look returned to me. She hesitated for quite a time before she spoke.

"May I ask you something? Just between ourselves?"

"Do, please."

"Was there a woman mixed up in it?"

"Not as far as we can tell. No harm in telling you what happened, at least as far as we know. You'll probably be able to read all about it tomorrow."

I gave her the outlines and all at once her mouth was agape again. It was after I'd mentioned that the room had been booked by someone calling himself Corland.

"Humbert Corland? That's who he went to see!"

"Humbert Corland?" I'd read that registration form too quickly and had taken the Christian name for Hubert. Now something was suddenly familiar. "Isn't he an author? I seem to remember my wife telling me to read a book of his."

"That would probably be *The Flying Beacon*," she said. "But let me tell you about it. It was this morning and Gordon came bursting into my room. He said Humbert Corland had just rung him to say he was very dissatisfied with the English handling of his books and he'd like a switch. He was at Liverpool, on his way to London, and he'd ring again later."

"Did he?"

"I don't know," she said. "I didn't go back to the office after lunch. I had to see a client, for one thing, and then I was having tea with an American publisher."

"A good bit of business, would it have been, if you'd managed to get this Corland?"

"A magnificent piece of business. He's one of the really coming men. Writes the George Birmingham sort of stuff, only better. He's selling big already and he's going to sell really big."

"Who handles him at the moment?"

"Laurie Demaine. He's Irish too, like Corland."

"It fits in," I said. "The Corland who took the room registered as coming from Belfast. You don't happen to have a reference book here so that I could look up his address?"

"Not here. There's one, of course, at the office."

I didn't like asking her, but it seemed that I would have to. Would she mind going to the office? A lot might depend on it, and the sooner we knew a whole lot about Corland the better.

"Not a bit," she said, "if it's going to help."

It took some time to find a taxi and it was about ten o'clock when we got to Brent Street. I told the taxi to wait. A couple of minutes later we had the address.

"Mind if we have a look in Posfort's office?"

I didn't think she quite liked the idea, but we went there all the same. On his desk was the same book of reference, but with a paper marking the page on which was Corland's name.

On that paper were a whole lot of figures, and a Belfast telephone number.

"Looks as if he'd been making some enquiries of his own," I said. "This is almost certainly Corland's number. What do you think the figures are?"

She frowned for a moment as she looked at them.

"Probably Corland's sales."

I put the paper in my wallet and we went back to the street.

"Just one thing," I said, as we came to the door. "In the morning this place will probably be turned upside down by the police. Probably nothing will be in the early morning papers, so don't mention a thing yourself."

She didn't say a word and I couldn't see her face in the comparative dark.

"May I say something else?" I went on. "I might be able to handle this end of things myself, but whether I do or not, tell the whole truth about everything you know. It always pays in the long run."

I'd expected her to protest, but she still didn't say a word, and it was not till I was showing her into the taxi that I knew why, for she had her handkerchief at her eyes, and I merely mumbled good night and a thank-you as I closed the door. I paid the driver and in a minute or two was hopping a bus that would get me near the Embankment.

Wharton was in his room and he hardly gave me time to get through the door.

"Got anything?"

"The telephone number of the man who booked that room," I told him. "Corland's the name. Try to get hold of someone there straight away. It's fairly late, but someone might be up."

He rang down. While we waited I told him what I had learned about Corland and his connection with Posfort.

"It fits in," I said. "Corland was sufficiently important for Posfort to have gone to see him and not the other way round. Also Corland mightn't have known just what kind of hotel the Royalty was, or else he thought it quite a fine place compared with the general run of Irish hotels."

The buzzer went. George picked up the receiver. It was not till a good five minutes later that he managed to put it down and nine-tenths of the time had been taken up with a spate of words that I could almost make out from where I sat.

George let out a breath, then gave me a glare.

"You got the hang of that?"

"Yes," I said. "It was Corland himself."

"Never heard of Posfort in his life! Hasn't been away from Belfast all day and can produce fifty people to prove it! Never had the faintest idea of changing his agent!" He paused for a breath. "Well, what do you make of that?"

"Just what you make of it yourself," I said. "Posfort was lured to that room by someone using Corland's name."

"Where's that get us?"

What could I do but shrug my shoulders?

George gave a grunt or two and began filling his pipe. It looked to me as if he had something on his mind and wasn't too happy about getting it out.

"Plenty of time yet," I said. "It's only four hours since Posfort was shot."

"Yes," he said. "That shooting. It gave me an idea. I don't think a lot of it, but we might have to consider it."

"Any idea's a good one till it's proved otherwise, George."

"Yes," he said. "What I was wondering was if Posfort had got himself mixed up in some way with those Irish madmen who've been giving trouble stealing ammunition and arms. Members of the Irish Republican Army, or whatever they call themselves."

"It could be," I said. "I'll know more tomorrow when I've run that Brent Street office through a small-toothed comb. That is, if you want me to take on that job."

"Of course you'll do it," he told me. "You know people there, don't you? You speak the lingo. Got any other ideas tonight, by the way?"

"Only one," I said, "and that might be important. I rather think Posfort once had an affair with that Lilian Rome I was telling you about. She must have been a highly presentable woman when he first went there. It's more than likely he climbed up on her shoulders."

"Pretty much of a Don Juan, wasn't he?" The look he gave was like a dirty story.

"He got around," I said. "Still, we'll know more by this time tomorrow. Any chance of Matthews being with me? Just in case the screws have to be put on?"

He thought that could be arranged. I suggested Brent Street at ten o'clock. He stared at that. Half the damn day would be gone.

"That's when the place opens," I said. "Unless you'd like us to get there earlier and admire the views."

3
INTO THE TUNNEL

I RANG Lilian Rome at about nine o'clock the next morning and told her what was going to happen. I painted Matthews as something of an ogre and said she mustn't be deceived by his seeming inconsequence. That was merely a trick to entrap the unwary. I added that we'd not be with her till a quarter-past ten to the dot, and she might arrange to have us shown straight in.

What Matthews and I did was to have coffee and a bun and a brief conference to pass the quarter of an hour. In our job you never know when the next meal is likely to come. He was mightily amused when I told him what I'd said of him. Matthews is a good man, but he couldn't have worked for years with Gorge Wharton if he hadn't retained a sense of humour and a capacity for patience. He's good-looking, too, is Matthews: just under six feet, dark-haired and with a faint smile that seems on the edge of a grin. Maybe that last is because he's still a bachelor. Wharton boasts of his own way with women witnesses: I'd as soon put my money on Matthews—if Wharton ever gave him a free hand.

I'd briefed him while we were having that coffee and it was he who began the questioning in Lilian Rome's office. What he wanted was a complete history of Gordon Posfort.

Old Mr. Holt was his only relative, she said, and he had died a year or two ago. Posfort had come to the firm through old Mr. Drench, who was also now dead. His widow was a kind of sleeping director. Clark, an original partner, had been killed in the blitz and his interests had been bought out.

"Just how did Posfort come to get on so well?" Matthews asked her.

"Well, he was very competent and he soon fitted in. He had quite a lot of connections and he brought in quite a lot of new business. Mr. Drench thought a great deal of him."

"And you, Miss Rome: how long have you been here?"

"All my life," she said. "I came here as Mr. Drench's secretary. I became a director after Mr. Clark died."

He gave her a grin.

"Well, I won't ask you your age. I'll try and work things out later."

"I make no secret of it," she told him. "I'm actually fifty-one."

"I won't believe that till I've proved it. But to get back to Posfort. Would I be right in saying that no-one here knows as much about him as yourself?"

Her face flushed slightly at that.

"Yes," she said. "The third director is our accountant and he joined us only two years ago."

"I see. And tell us frankly. Just what did you think of Posfort? As a man, not a colleague."

She didn't hesitate.

"I'm afraid I knew very little of him except as a colleague. He was a much younger man—only forty-two—and after office hours we had our own interests."

"Let's be blunt," he said. "Our information is that he was very much of a ladies' man."

That seemed to shake her a bit.

"Just what do you mean?"

"He means what he said," I put in. "He liked women in his life. He was the sort who *had* to have a woman around. He never married again, did he, after his wife divorced him?"

"No. He didn't."

"Ever have any trouble about women in this office?"

Her face flushed again and she tried to turn it into indignation.

"How dare you make such suggestions! He's dead, and surely common decency—"

"Now, now, now," broke in Matthews, and it might have been Wharton himself speaking. "You were told that everything was confidential. There'll have to be an inquest, you know, so which would you rather do? Talk to us quietly here or have to give evidence in public?"

"I can only tell what I know."

"Very well," I said. "Suppose you tell us what you know about him and Caroline Halsing."

"I knew nothing."

"Well, that's less definite than saying there *was* nothing. Tell us what you suspected."

She fidgeted with the papers on her desk. She let out a breath.

"Very well. I thought he was turning her head."

"And that's all?"

"That's all."

"Then let me put it another way. You weren't afraid that he might marry her. What you were afraid of was that you knew he wasn't the marrying kind and that she wasn't that sort of girl."

"Well . . . perhaps, yes."

"That's that, then," I said. "What we want now is every possible detail about her. You've probably got some records here."

She knew everything herself, she said, and there was no need to consult records. Matthews began taking everything down. Caroline Halsing had been educated at a high-class private school in Kent, had taken a course in what might be called secretaryship and at just over eighteen had applied for a job with a doctor. She was with him for about five years, then had come to Drench and Posfort. Her home address was The Rectory, Ralehurst, Kent, but she had rooms of her own at 54 Playton Street, Camden Town. She was believed to go home for most week-ends.

"Her sister, by the way, is Bridget Halsing, the actress."

"Really?" I said. "I knew the name was familiar."

"Bridget's husband is an actor—Courtney Haze."

"Good lord!" I said. "They're both very important people. There was some talk about Haze being given a knighthood. Probably that'll be coming later. Know where they live?"

"Very well indeed," she said. "I lunched there about a year ago with Caroline. Twenty-three Quinton Place, Westminster."

"That's fine," I said. "But that dreadful suicide business. It was a great shock to you."

"A very great shock."

"Did you by any chance impute the cause of it to Posfort?"

"Why should I? In any case I had nothing but suspicions to go on."

"I understand that she left of her own accord. What did Posfort say about it to you?"

"Well, it was curious. He wouldn't talk about it. He got quite angry. If she wants to leave, let her leave—that sort of thing."

That seemed to exhaust the subject of Caroline Halsing. Matthews took over.

"As to who might have wanted to kill Posfort, Miss Rome, would it be too fantastic to think of some client he'd offended?"

She smiled, and it might have been from relief.

"More than fantastic."

Nobody could have been more staggered when he told her the truth about Corland. As for any suggestion of Posfort's having made enemies of the Southern Irish, that, she said, was too preposterous for words.

"Where did Posfort live?" he asked her.

She must have known that we could find that information in the telephone directory. Wharton had, in fact, gone to his flat the previous night. What Matthews wanted, apparently, was to see how quickly she answered, though again there was no point in it. After years of association together, his address must have been as familiar as her own—and his telephone number.

"Flat 22, Lancing House, Newton Hill," she said. "That's near Ealing, if you didn't know."

"And his solicitors?"

"The same as our own, unless he changed them recently. Harries, Son and Harries, 15 Giles Court. That's just off Chancery Lane."

He closed his notebook.

"That's almost all, except that we shall probably have to ask you for a formal statement later. But I'd like to ask you a question. Something you can really help us about. This killing depended on enticing Posfort to a certain room in that hotel by a pretence of being a certain Humbert Corland. Doesn't that make it a certainty that the one who killed him must have had considerable knowledge about a literary agency?"

She stared.

"You mean someone here?"

"It's a possibility. Something we can't afford to overlook. Just what is your staff here?"

"Well, there was Gordon Posfort and myself, and we each had our own secretaries. Miss Barnes, his secretary, also acts as receptionist. Mr. Forrest, the accountant, has his own clerk, then there's a pool of two typists on whom any of us can draw." She smiled. "Surely you see that nobody here could have been concerned in anything so dreadful as a murder?"

"You all got on well together? You were a happy family?"

"I think so. My own secretary's been with me for over eight years. Typists come and go, but I think everyone's as happy as in any office."

"What about Miss Barnes? I mean, what's your opinion of her?"

"Well, she seems to have settled down pretty well."

"You don't like her, do you?" I asked bluntly.

She gave me a wary look.

"I have very little to do with her."

"Mind if we have her in here, just to ask her a question or two? You tell her who we are and that we're on business to do with Mr. Posfort."

She buzzed through. A couple of minutes and Hilda Barnes was coming in. There was no smile on her face till she caught sight of us. Me she recognised. Maybe she thought I was a client.

"Yes, Miss Rome?"

Lilian Rome explained. The smile went again. I began the questioning.

"Would I be right in saying, Miss Barnes, that you were very much in Mr. Posfort's confidence?"

"You mean about . . . business?"

"Yes, and possibly his private affairs too."

"Oh, but no." The smile was most winsome. "Why should I know about his private affairs?"

"Of course not. How foolish of me. He never took you out anywhere? Say, to a dinner and a show?"

The look was long and level. With it there was a little fear.

"Just what do you mean?"

"Just a simple question." I shrugged my shoulders. "Did he or did he not ever take you out to dinner?"

"Of course not! Why should he?"

"I can think of various reasons," I told her. "But why did you tell me a lie? You did dine with him. You were at the Cap d'Argent dining with him in an upstairs room last Monday night."

"Who told you that?"

"It's our business to know things. What we don't know we find out. So don't you think you'd better tell us the truth? Answer this question, for instance; what did Posfort tell you about Caroline Halsing, your predecessor?"

"He didn't tell me anything."

I got to my feet.

"Better get your hat and coat." I turned to Matthews. "We'll have her questioned at the Yard."

"No," she said. "No. He didn't tell me anything, really he didn't. Only why she left."

"And why did she leave?"

"He said she'd got too big for her job."

"I see. And he interviewed you for your job?"

"Yes. There were several of us, really."

I let my eyes run slowly over her.

"And he chose you. And before you'd been here very long you were dining out together. Ever go to his flat?"

"If I did there was no harm in it."

"Glad to hear it. Very well, Miss Barnes. We've finished with you—for the moment. If Miss Rome doesn't want you, you may go. But just one other thing: where were you at seven o'clock last night?"

"At home," she said. "Well, not at home. We went next door to their television."

She went. I asked Lilian Rome to give me her address. "You hate the sight of her, don't you? May I tell you why? Correct me if I'm wrong, but you saw her going the way that Caroline Halsing went. But you liked Caroline. That's why you were so shocked at her death. This one you didn't care about. You just despised her."

She didn't speak. Matthews got to his feet.

"May I use your telephone, Miss Rome? I take it I shan't be overheard. No need for you to leave. In fact I'd rather you stayed."

He dialled the Yard and asked to be put through to Wharton. Wharton spoke almost at once.

"Matthews here, sir. That secretary who committed suicide had rooms at 54 Playton Street, Camden Town. Might someone go there at once to check up on her weekends? We know her home address and we can counter-check there. And a secretary here called Hilda Barnes of 3 Wallace Avenue, Highbury . . . claims to have been next door watching television, if you'd like to check up."

He replaced the receiver and got to his feet again.

"You knew Miss Halsing's rooms, Miss Rome?"

"Yes," she said. "I went there more than once. They were very nice rooms. The landlady was actually a former house-maid who'd been with her family."

"You never thought of warning her against Posfort?"

She moistened her lips.

"I did once tell her not to take him too seriously. But you couldn't possibly imagine her doing anything that was—well, just not right."

That was all, or nearly so. We were at the door when it opened suddenly and a man came in. He was holding a newspaper and looking perturbed.

"Oh!" he said, and backed away again at the sight of us.

"That your Mr. Forrest?" I asked. "If so, he seems to have heard about Posfort's death."

We said goodbye at the outer door.

"Just a final question," Matthews said. "You don't open on Saturdays?"

"Oh no."

"Not even for any of the staff when you happen to be rushed?"

She said they never were so rushed as that.

We took a bus at Ludgate Hill and went upstairs. I asked Matthews what he thought of things. He used rather a vulgar word about Hilda Barnes.

"That Miss Rome gets me, though," he said. "I still think whoever did the job must have been right in the know. No-one else could have worked that Corland stunt."

"You think she did it?"

"Well, there's a motive," he said. "You claim she'd once had an affair with him and then he'd given her the chuck for some-one else. Perhaps there were one or two someone elses till he got hold of the Halsing girl. She was different. She was a personal friend of Rome's. I'll bet you anything you like that she knows why the Halsing girl committed suicide, and that it was on account of Posfort. Then she saw him starting in on that blonde tart and it was too much for her. And I'll bet you a fiver that she's fixed herself some sort of alibi for yesterday evening."

"Maybe you're right," I said, "but aren't we forgetting one thing? Suppose there's quite another reason for the suicide? Suppose Caroline left a note giving quite another reason?"

"I don't quite get you."

"Well, what are we after? We're enquiring into Caroline Halsing's death and hoping to make Posfort's killer someone who was out for revenge. But if there was nothing to avenge—what then?"

"Plenty of time yet," he told me. "All the same, I'm pretty damn-sure, and so is the Super, that it *was* revenge. It wasn't a simple killing. Someone meant him to die a pretty painful death."

I thought that out for a minute or two. Six bullets had been pumped into Posfort, as I had learned from Matthews. They hadn't gone through the body because they were from a 6.35 mm. Italian Feroni, a smallish gun that, pressed against Posfort's stomach, would have made very little noise.

How could Lilian Rome have got such a gun? Better still, *who* could have got such a gun?

The thoughts were like furtive fingers, groping in the dark. Something else emerged.

"Mind if we get off at Trafalgar Square?" I said. "I'd like to consult a bookseller I know."

There were quite a few people in that shop and we had to go right through to find the proprietor at the far end. I asked his opinion of Humbert Corland and he confirmed what Lilian Rome had told me.

"He's already a well-known name?"

"Most decidedly."

"Got a copy of his latest?"

"If you mean *The Flying Beacon*, I haven't. Sold right out. There might be some more in, though, on Monday."

"A pity," I said. "I badly wanted to see a copy."

"If it's just to see it," he said, "I can show you my own. I always keep a first edition of anything that's likely to appreciate in value."

He brought out his copy from the bottom drawer of his desk. I wasn't interested in the book itself, but the jacket. It had just what I wanted. On the back was a photograph of Corland—a youngish, earnest-looking man with an incipient but untidy moustache and glasses, and with something which to me was definitely Irish about his face. The short biography beneath it said that he had been born in Belfast and had lived there all his life. It gave a quote from the publisher's reader—"When I'd finished the MS. I knew I'd had the experience of a lifetime." It added that the ordinary reader would think so too after reading the book. Humbert Corland, it concluded, had more than arrived.

"Well, what did you make of it?" I asked Matthews as we walked on down Whitehall.

"You tell me," he said. "That sort of thing is rather above my head."

"Then let me put myself in the murderer's place," I told him. "I want to kill Posfort and the obvious way to get at him is through his job. He has to be lured somewhere where he'll be anxious to go and where I can make a safe getaway. The best way to entice him is through a mythical client. But I happen to be looking at new books on a bookstall or in a shop and I see *The Flying Beacon*. On the back of the jacket is all I want. I'd have preferred an American author who was supposed to be in England on a trip, but an Irish author would do at a pinch, especially if I claim to be on my way from Liverpool, so that he can't get into touch with me. That, as I see it, is how the murderer might have arrived at what he did. If I'm right, then we have to change our ideas. The murderer needn't have been anyone at Brent Street. Anyone with an elementary knowledge of authors and literary agents would fill the bill."

He looked so glum that I had to laugh. By then we were cutting through to the Yard. A minute or two later we were in Wharton's room. A blast of fug hit us and the room was blue with smoke.

I'd thought he'd be disappointed with what we had to tell him, but he wasn't; at least he didn't even hint that we'd been wasting our time.

"Looks as if it's beginning to fit in," he told us. "The Old Gent"—that's the hypocritically deprecating way in which he likes to allude to himself—"hasn't been asleep. She didn't commit suicide at Camden Town. She was staying with an aunt at Winchester. Died from an overdose of sleeping tablets. I've asked to have the coroner put into touch with me.

"Anything for me to do?"

"Better get yourself a meal and be back in an hour," he said. "I have an idea you may be going down to that Ralehurst place. You're a better hand than I at talking to parsons."

I didn't disillusion him. Downstairs I looked up the Rev. Timothy Halsing and found he was a Cambridge man, though not from my college. I also looked up a route and decided to turn off short of Orpington. With any luck the trip should not take much more than half an hour. Then I had a meal at a pub in Masters Street and was back just inside the hour. George had had his meal brought in on a tray and he was just pushing the bell for the debris to go. He looked mightily pleased.

"Just as I guessed," he told me. "That Caroline Halsing was two months gone." He waited for the applause. "Well, what're you looking so miserable about?"

"Was I?" I couldn't tell him that for me it was almost a personal tragedy and shame. Even the thought of Posfort under that blanket didn't cheer me.

"You certainly haven't been idle," I told him. "That was confidential, about the pregnancy?"

"It didn't need to be brought out at the inquest. She left a note for her aunt which was produced in court. The coroner also told me that she'd written two letters that last evening and had gone out to post them. That's one thing you might find out at Ralehurst—if one was for the father. I reckon the other'd be for Posfort, and I hope it made the swine squirm."

"Anything from the landlady?"

"Only that for about her last twelve months she never spent a single weekend at Camden Town. You can check that at Ralehurst, too."

"Matthews with me, or do I go alone?"

"He's on his way to Winchester," he told me. "We might unearth some more. You'll do better on your own. You've got that sort of gift of the gab." I don't think he saw me wince. "Better take a police car and driver. It'll look more impressive."

4
AT THE RECTORY

I DIDN'T set off at once for Ralehurst. Downstairs I rang Lilian Rome.

"Ludovic Travers, Miss Rome. Sorry to bother you again so soon, but if a certain suicide took place at Winchester, how did you know about it? My information is that everything was rather hushed up."

"My nephew happened to see her there," she said. "He'd met her here and knew her well."

"Yes, but about the suicide."

"Well, Martin's in the Navy and he was back at sea when it happened, but my sister lives near Winchester and she sent him a copy of the local newspaper and she sent me one too."

"I've got you. And your nephew's still at sea?"

"Well, no. He's actually coming to see me tomorrow. I'm taking him out to lunch and we are going to a matinée."

"Fine. But just one other thing. We discussed the possibility of a certain man's connection with that Winchester affair. Have you any reason to suspect that any member of her family had the same idea?"

She hesitated.

"Not an actual member of the family."

"Well, who?" I asked her impatiently.

"Courtney Haze. I believe he came here to see—to see you-know-who about it."

"Look," I said. "This is strictly between ourselves, but I'm just going down to Ralehurst myself. I've got to see you this evening—and your nephew."

"But how—"

"Don't say it can't be done," I told her. "It's got to be done. If he isn't in town, you must get him here. At eight o'clock, shall we say, at your flat?"

"Well, I'll try."

"That's fine," I said. "Believe me, it's for your own good. Neither of you wants to be mixed up in an inquest."

It took well over the time I'd thought to get to Ralehurst, for traffic was bad through the suburbs as far as the bypass. It was quite a tiny village. Against the church was the rectory: one of those Georgian buildings whose upkeep should have been a nightmare to an incumbent, but when we came up to it I knew that Halsing must have money of his own, for the place had nothing about it of the unkempt. A slightly pre-war Morris saloon was standing in the drive just short of the porch and our car drew in behind it.

A youngish maid in neat black opened the door. I asked if I could see Mr. Halsing.

"This way, sir," she said, with never a word or question as to who I was. I stepped into an entrance hall and she crossed it to a door on the left and showed me into a smallish room that was obviously a study.

"If you'll wait here, sir, I'll tell Mr. Halsing you've arrived."

"Just a minute," I said, and gave her a smile. "How did he know I was coming?"

"I don't know, sir," she said. "All I was told was when you came to show you straight in the study."

"Well, in case there's some mistake, you'd better give Mr. Halsing this card."

She took it, gave me a rather anxious look, and went. I took one of the old-fashioned chairs and looked round. It was the usual rectorial study: a desk over which was a calendar with the name of a religious society, books—ecclesiastical mostly—in a quite nice Chippendale case, and on the walls some Medici prints of Italian primitives. A reproduction oriental rug covered most of the floor and there was a dull fire in the tiny grate.

The door opened suddenly and Halsing came in. He was a tall, handsome-looking man with a rather aesthetic face that reminded me of Forbes-Robertson. His eyes were crinkling at the sight of me, but I don't think he really smiled.

"Please don't get up, Mr. Travers." His voice was beautifully modulated. "I hope I haven't kept you waiting too long."

I assured him he hadn't kept me more than a minute.

"Do smoke, please, if you wish. I'm afraid I don't smoke myself, but I'm quite used to it."

"Not at the moment," I said. "I'm here, as you may have guessed, on very distressing business. In fact it's going to be hard for me to tell you exactly why I *am* here."

He drew up a chair to face my own. If his look had ever been welcoming it had suddenly ceased to be so.

"The fact that I am what I am, Mr. Travers, makes me used to what you call distressing business. Just what is it you wish to see me about?"

"Perhaps you'll be so good as to answer a question first. Everything said here, by the way, is in the strictest confidence, but have you learned about the death—the murder—of a man named Posfort?"

"Yes," he told me evenly. "A friend just brought me the news."

I wasn't feeling happy; not because of what I would have to say but because of that isolation in which he suddenly seemed to be wrapping himself. It was as if I were under the microscope—not he.

"Someone murdered Posfort," I said, "and we have to find the one who did it. We start with motives, Mr. Halsing. Does that tell you why I'm here?"

The thin lips took quite a time to unclamp.

"Would you explain yourself further? Please don't consider my feelings."

I told him practically all we knew, and his eyes hardly blinked and the thin lips never unclamped.

"We consider, therefore, we have every reason to question every member of your family. It's almost a certainty that nothing will come of it, but it has to be done. All of you must have wished the man Posfort some sort of punishment for the damnable thing he did."

"My dear sir, must you indulge in homiletics? What you're telling me in so many words is that a member of my family might have killed him. You wish to question us?"

It was hard to show sympathy or even to be urbane. That detachment, that near omniscience, was beginning to irritate me.

"Either confidentially beforehand," I said, "or publicly at Posfort's inquest. With your co-operation, that's something we hope to avoid. What was in that letter your daughter wrote you on her last evening, Mr. Halsing?"

"That," he told me slowly, "is something between myself and my daughter—my late daughter."

"You have that letter?"

"I destroyed it."

"It mentioned Posfort as responsible for her condition?"

"It did not."

I let out a breath.

"I must say that you're not being very helpful. If you prefer something more direct, what about your own alibi for last night at seven o'clock?"

"I must decline to answer that," he told me evenly.

"You think it an insult to your cloth?"

He wasn't listening to me, but to the sudden noise of a car. That study window faced the side gardens and I couldn't see the car, but almost at once I heard a man's voice saying not to wait, and then a thank-you-sir and the car—or taxi—moving round.

"Will you pardon me for just a moment," Halsing said and was getting to his feet.

"By all means."

But he had already gone. I sat on for three or four minutes and what was disturbing me was not that lack of co-operation on his part, for he had seemed to me to have tacitly admitted that it had been Posfort who was responsible for the death of his daughter. What did worry me was the fact that he had known that I was coming, and the only one who could have warned him, or advised him, seemed to be Wharton. And if George had rung him, then I couldn't see why. It took away the whole element of surprise: in fact it seemed the last thing that should have been done. And when I did have another idea I didn't have time to pursue it, for the door was opening again.

"I'm so sorry. Would you care to come into the drawing-room? My son-in-law's just arrived and perhaps you'd care to see him."

The tone had been much milder. I followed him across the hall and he ushered me through a door to a beautifully proportioned room. With the experience of one who has merely dabbled a good deal in antiques I was aware of the old-fashioned water-colour drawings and the silk pictures on the walls, and the Queen Anne bureau-bookcase and, beyond me, the blazing fire in the handsome basket grate. Two fine Dresden conversation groups were on the mantelpiece and above them hung an eighteenth-century portrait of a divine—probably a Romney. Ralehurst Rectory, I thought to myself, was not without money.

"Courtney, I don't think you know Mr. Travers."

"Oh, but I do," said Courtney Haze, and he was smiling as he held out his hand. "This is my brother, Roland, by the way. Do sit down, won't you?"

I'd seen Courtney Haze scores of times on the stage or in films, but there was nothing of the actor about him at that moment, unless it was a superb self-possession. His brother was younger and only slightly like him, though the moustache might have had something to do with that. Halsing took a chair rather in the background and I sensed at once that it was to be Courtney Haze who would be in command.

"I saw you at the Old Bailey some time back," he said. "You were giving evidence in the Vinton case. I was about to do something of the kind myself in *Martha's Husband*, and I found you most useful."

"I saw you in the play," I told him, "but I didn't spot myself. I didn't see the film."

"The play's just finished," he said, "as you probably know, and I'm having a bit of a holiday before rehearsals."

"And your wife? I admire her enormously too."

"Bridget? She's still in *Two Times Two*. That's probably going on for ever."

"You don't mind me saying it"—that was the quiet voice of his brother—"but you don't look much like a detective."

I smiled as I brought out my warrant card.

"Oh, I don't mean that. I mean—"

"He means what he said," Courtney told me, "that you don't look like a copper."

"Even the Yard moves with the times," I told them amiably. "Some of us are less obvious than the others."

Halsing cut in there.

"I've mentioned your business this afternoon and I'm wondering if you'd care to come to the point."

"Yes," Courtney said. "Apparently you want to question us."

I went over the whole thing again and his eyes never left my face. His brother had his face turned towards the fire and he turned back only when I had to put the somewhat abrupt question.

"So, you see, I'd like a definite answer from someone. Perhaps you'll supply it, Mr. Haze. Was or was not Posfort responsible for your sister-in-law's death?"

"This is confidential, you said?"

"Strictly so—at the moment." I smiled. "Naturally if you were to tell me that you'd killed Posfort, then it couldn't stay so."

"I didn't kill him," he said. "Frankly, I'd have done so with the greatest pleasure in the world—if I could have got away with it."

"That answers the question," I told him, and turned to his brother. "What about you, Mr. Haze? Had you any reason to feel the same?"

"Perhaps, yes," he said quietly. "I knew Caroline pretty well: in fact I'd once hoped to marry her. As it was, I was a kind of elder brother." His smile was apologetic. "I'm telling you that because you'd probably find it out."

"That's very frank," I said. "If I can have both your alibis for last night at seven o'clock, which is when Posfort was killed, then neither of you will be troubled again." I turned to Courtney. "You, Mr. Haze?"

"Well, I think I can satisfy you. I was actually watching my wife's show—a sort of busman's holiday. The play begins at seven prompt and my wife saw me there. She's on, as you know, when the curtain goes up."

"And you, Mr. Haze?"

"I was at Marland, about twenty miles from here. That's where I live. It's well over half an hour from Town."

"And you were actually doing what?"

"Well, I had to look in at a British Legion concert in the village. I was a bit late—five minutes or so after seven o'clock—and I had to go early." He smiled. "Between ourselves, I'm not frightfully keen on concerts."

A minute or two and I was putting away my notebook. "That seems absolutely satisfactory. I'm sorry you had to be troubled, but I'm under orders as you probably guess. Just one other thing. As a matter of red-tape, the alibis will have to be checked. I may speak to Mrs. Haze?"

"Why not, my dear fellow?"

And so to his brother.

"Anyone I can check with about you, Mr. Haze?"

"I don't know," he said. "I sat next to a Mrs. Kinter, who keeps our general stores, and I did just give something to the rector. I think both will give me a clean bill. At least, for seven o'clock."

I closed my notebook again and rose.

"I'm more than grateful to both of you. I don't expect you'll be hearing from us again."

"You will have some tea?"

That, surprisingly, was Halsing.

"Thank you, no, sir. I'd like to get back before any mist comes on."

I shook hands with the two Hazes and turned back to follow Halsing to the door. Then that door fairly burst open, and a man of about thirty came in, and he was flourishing a newspaper. There was a look of Halsing about him.

"Have you heard—"

He stopped short at the sight of me.

"We *have* heard," cut in Halsing almost angrily. "That is if you mean about the death of that man Posfort." He turned to me. "This, Mr. Travers, is James, my son."

"How d'you do," James Halsing said.

"Mr. Travers is from Scotland Yard," his father said. "Also both Courtney and Roland brought newspapers, so you see we're well informed. Mr. Travers has been asking questions."

"Haven't I seen you before?" James said.

"It's possible," I said, "but I doubt it. But perhaps I can remove you from the list too. Let me explain."

A minute or two and he was giving his alibi. It wasn't worth a great deal, as I had to tell him, for it was merely a visit to a cinema at Orpington.

"No-one saw you there?"

"Should they?"

"Don't be flippant, James," Courtney told him sharply. "It's damn-bad manners."

"I don't see it. Here I'm being virtually suspected—"

"Oh, shut up!" That was Roland. The voice had been quiet but incisive. "Can't you answer a perfectly simple question?"

"I suppose so, and without your help. No-one saw me," he told me, "if that's what you want to know. All I can do is tell you about the picture. Oh, yes, and there was the cinema-park attendant. I tipped him when I took my motorbike."

"That would be when?"

"About half-past eight."

"I'm very grateful to you," I said. "Now I'll be getting along."

Courtney was suddenly there.

"I'll show Mr. Travers out, sir. I have to go out in any case."

Halsing held out his hand in goodbye, but there was still something hostile in his look. Courtney Haze and I went out to the car and he halted just short of his brother's Morris. It wasn't cold standing there, though dusk was already in the sky.

"How'd you get on with my father-in-law?" he asked me.

I smiled.

"Well, he wasn't exactly communicative."

"You've got to go easy with him," he told me. "That business of Caroline nearly killed him. She was the apple of his eye, you know. Mind you, he never was exactly a riot of fun, but he could be very pleasant, and genial. Now he's sort of shrivelled up."

"Why did he seem so disinterested in Posfort's death?"

"Just because he *isn't* interested," he said. "It's Caroline he's thinking of. What's happened to Posfort won't bring her back. You didn't know Caroline—"

"I knew her by sight."

"You did!"

I told him what I knew of her and how delightful I had always found her. His only comment was a wonder why I should be keen on finding who had killed Posfort.

"Frankly, if I could put a spoke in your wheel I would. If I knew the fellow who did it I'd do my damnedest to see him in the clear."

"All the same," I told him, "that won't stop you from telling me one or two things I want to know. What's James, your brother-in-law, do for a living?"

"James? He's just got an M.C. in Malaya. He's home on a couple of months' leave. A harum-scarum sort of chap. You mustn't take him too seriously."

"Much of his leave gone?"

"About five weeks. Strictly between ourselves, he and Caroline were remarkably fond of each other. The rector rather let out that Caroline said in that last letter she wrote him that James was one of the people she couldn't face. That seems to be why she did what she did before he got home."

That was all. He shook hands and said we must lunch at the Garrick some time, and he'd give me a ring. He gave me a wave of the hand as the car circled round, and I looked back to see him still standing there as we went through the gate. I wondered what our parting would have been like if I had told him that James Halsing was the man I'd seen the previous night peering round the corner and along the short corridor at the end of which was Room 323.

I sat at the back of the car because I wanted to think. That visit had been exploratory—a kind of reconnaissance—but it had produced plenty of ideas, and ideas were the things that mattered. The Yard doesn't pounce indiscriminately, it takes its time. It's the nearest thing I know to the mills of God: it grinds slowly but exceedingly small. Even in that matter of James Halsing it would not pounce till Wharton was ready.

But what about James Halsing? By harum-scarum his brother-in-law had probably meant reckless to the point of lunacy: though that did not detract from the merit of what he had done in Malaya. Nowadays they don't give away M.C.s in Christmas crackers. And if it was he who had killed Posfort, would that recklessness and indifference to danger explain why he had stayed near the scene of the killing for almost half an hour after that killing had been done? Somehow I couldn't quite believe it.

Then what about that testimony of the chambermaid? Had two men been concerned? Was James Halsing one of them, and had he stayed on to cover in some way the tracks of his accomplice? Again I couldn't quite believe it. All the same, if there had been two men, what combination could they be of the men I'd seen that afternoon?

What of the Rev. Timothy Halsing? No-one could conceivably believe that he could have made himself an instrument of justice. The fact that he looked like an Edwardian actor didn't make him one, and all I had seen in his taciturnity and self-repression had been the shattering grief about which Courtney Haze had told me. No divine wrath and no thundering condemnations: Posfort's name, as I remember, he had never even mentioned.

What of Courtney Haze? And need the confederate have been a man? Mightn't his wife swear to that alibi of his because she knew exactly on what he had been engaged? He was an actor. His voice might have been that of the Corland who had booked the room, and he could have made himself up to some close resemblance of that photograph of Corland on the jacket of a book. Had James Halsing been in it too? Or had he had suspicions and had been at the Royalty merely as the Peeping Tom that he had looked?

What of Roland Haze? Why had he told me so frankly that he had once hoped to marry Caroline Halsing? But he had added that he had settled down to being merely a kind of elder brother, which had been as much as telling me not to get ideas into my head. Had it been necessary for him to tell me anything at all, except the details of the alibi for which I'd asked? I didn't know. I did know that he had spoken with an amused acceptance of my presence. But he also had a definite individuality, even if, like his brother and everyone else connected with Caroline, he would stir never a finger to help find the man who had killed Posfort. I had liked the way he had put James Halsing in his place. The two Hazes, when I came to think back, had acted very much together, even if Roland—I put his age as the middle thirties—had let his brother do most of the talking. Courtney, of course, was nearer fifty than forty. But all that was no clue to any supposed alliance of the two brothers in the matter of killing Posfort.

When I walked into Wharton's room that evening I had little of importance to report except that matter of James Halsing.

"Before we decide about him, let me get something clear," Wharton said. "The parson hadn't heard about the murder. He heard of it from that Roland Haze, who came along specially in his car. Doesn't that strike you as unnecessary? Why couldn't he have telephoned?"

I didn't know. All I could suggest was that the news would mean more to the family—counting Roland as part of it—than we might perhaps appreciate.

"Then what about the Courtney one? He was sent for. Why should he have to come down from Town?"

"Town isn't so far," I said. "A few minutes to Orpington and then a taxi."

"Yes, but why the family conference? Posfort was dead. Why the devil should they want to argue about it? Unless"—he leaned across the desk and wagged a finger at me—"the whole lot of 'em were in it up to the neck. And there was the son. He comes bursting in with a newspaper. Why? Did he know what was going to be in the paper?"

"No use asking me, George," I said. "But what are you going to do about him?"

"Have him here at once," he said. "Just for a friendly chat. I'll get the local people to bring him in."

5
STILL THE TUNNEL

I JUST had time to dictate the report and snatch a meal at home, and then I had to find a taxi to get me to Lilian's flat. I couldn't help thinking again what a well-preserved woman she was, though even the best of corsetings couldn't conceal quite all the bulging. Her rather plump face didn't look so unreservedly friendly, in spite of the way she ushered me in.

"How nice to see you again. This is Martin, my nephew. Martin Collier."

"How d'you do, sir."

He was in mufti and he didn't look a day over twenty-five, for he had that boyish look of the young naval officer; the smooth, tanned cheeks and the clear eyes. It turned out that he was twenty-six, exactly the age of Caroline Halsing.

"You'll have a drink, sir?" He waved a hand towards the side table. "Whisky or—"

"Whisky would be very nice," I said. "Not too much and just a splash of soda."

"And you, Aunt?"

"Just a small whisky too, dear."

We all had whiskies and we lifted them and drank. It was cosy there in front of the electric fire, even if the room was just a bit too warm.

"Mind if I call you Lilian?" I asked her over my glass.

She smiled.

"I'd like you to."

"Well, then, Lilian, I've a small bone to pick with you. Why did you let Courtney Haze know that I was on my way to Ralehurst?"

"He told you so?"

"Don't let's beg the question," I told her, and friendlily enough. "As a matter of fact he didn't. It turned out to be a simple deduction. You told him and he told his father-in-law, and the whole family was practically waiting for me. Why'd you do it?"

She had flushed.

"Because I'd told you something I shouldn't. About Courtney Haze's visit to the office. To see Gordon."

"Well, perhaps you were right," I told her. "But about that visit. What actually took place? Or don't you know."

"I don't know," she said. "I just happened to be in the outer room when he came in. He said he'd like to see Gordon, so I took him along to my room and rang from there, and Gordon asked me what he wanted. Courtney had told me he wanted to see him on urgent private business, and Gordon told me he'd ring through when he was ready. Courtney and I had a chat—I told you I'd met him and his wife—and then Gordon rang. I was rather busy after that and when I called Gordon about an hour later he wasn't there, and Miss Barnes told me he and Courtney Haze had gone out. By the way, I fired her this morning. Paid her cash in lieu of notice."

"Not sorry to hear it," I said. "You said something to Gordon later?"

"Only to ask what Courtney Haze had wanted. He was quite snappy about it. Said it was something to do with an autobiography and it had fallen through."

"You didn't believe him?"

"I knew he was lying."

"Wonder why Courtney didn't give him a damn good hiding?" The smile was almost a sneer.

"Gordon could lie his way out of anything."

"Now you, young fellow," I said. "What do you know about things?"

"Not very much," he said. "It shook me pretty badly when I got the news of what she'd done. I just couldn't believe it. Or understand it."

Caroline hadn't been mentioned, so it was plain what was in his mind.

"You knew Caroline well?"

"Ever since she began working in Aunt's office. That was two years ago."

"You were in love with her?"

He wasn't looking at me but at the fire.

"Well, about a year ago I thought she'd get engaged to me, and then she suddenly began to change. Wouldn't take me seriously any longer, if you know what I mean. I did get her to go out with me once or twice, but there was nothing to it. I might have been going out with my own sister."

"Had you any reason to think she'd got attached to some other man?"

"As a matter of fact I did," he said. "I tackled her with it, but she was just maddening about it. Hinted and then took it back. That sort of thing. Oh, and something else. She began telling me I was too young. Inexperienced, and so on. What d'you think of that? I was the same age as her, and I told her so."

"That looks like a lead to Posfort," I said. "Know anything about a man called Roland Haze?"

"Oh, him!" he said. "Nothing serious there. He was far too old for her. He was a kind of relation. Her sister married his brother."

I smiled.

"Wait a minute, young fellow. Roland Haze can't be a day over thirty-five or six. That makes me a Methuselah. You really think he was too old for her?"

"Well, he was stuffy. He must have tons of money. He's a director of those marmalade people, Vargo, or something."

His look said that that ought to ring some sort of bell, but it didn't.

"What's money to do with it?"

"Well, he's stuffy. Lives in some village or other as if he hadn't got a penny."

"Some like it that way," I said. "But did Caroline say he was too old? I had an idea he used to be in love with her."

"Then he got over it long before I knew her," he said. "She regarded him as more like an uncle. He used to take her out sometimes, but just like an uncle. Or an elder brother."

"Did you ever meet him?"

"Once or twice," he said. "He was quite a nice chap. Quiet and—well, stuffy."

"I see. And what about your meeting Caroline in Winchester?"

"If you mean the last time I saw her"—his eyes turned away again—"all I can say is I was absolutely shocked at the sight of her, and she told me she'd been ill and was taking a holiday with her aunt. I wanted her to come and have some coffee with me, but she wouldn't. I hadn't got a lot of time, but I rang the house from Southampton the next day and the aunt told me she wasn't too well again and couldn't see anybody. I guess that's about all."

There was a heavy silence. I broke it.

"Suppose you'd known then what you know now. What would you have done to Posfort?"

"Done?" He looked round at me, brows knitted. "I'd have given him the hiding of his life, even if he was as big as a house. And I'd have done it in public. I'd have made such a stink that he'd have been ashamed to show his face in Town."

"But you didn't," I said. "You didn't even shoot him last night."

"No," he said. "But I'd like to shake hands with the one who did."

"Martin, don't say such things!"

"It's true, Aunt Lilian," he told her evenly, "so why be afraid to say it?"

"Where were you, actually, at seven o'clock last night?" I asked. "Just for the records."

"Yes," he said slowly. "That's different. As a matter of fact I'm not prepared to tell you."

"You must be joking."

"Oh no, I'm not. I'm simply not prepared to tell you. No one can make me tell you. I know I didn't kill him. I didn't even know he was dead till I saw a late morning paper."

I tried to point out the seriousness of what he was doing, but it made no difference. I had to leave it there and switch the talk back to Caroline and himself. But nothing new came of it and after some general chat I rose to go. Ten minutes later I was ringing Lilian Rome from a booth in the Underground.

"Travers, Lilian," I said. "But just prevaricate for once and don't let your nephew know."

"As a matter of fact he's gone," she said. "He left just after you did."

"Well, I don't think he had any hand in that business of last night," I told her. "It's purely a private reason why he won't talk. Apparently you got into touch with him this morning—"

"It was he who rang me."

"The point is, where from?"

There was a silence.

"That's queer," she said. "He didn't say where from. And I haven't asked him since. We just agreed to meet for lunch tomorrow and to do a show."

"Yes, but how did you get in touch with him so as to get him to your flat tonight?"

"Of course," she said. "I knew he sometimes stayed at the Chichester, just off Regent Street, so I rang him on chance, and he was there."

"That's fine," I said. "Don't worry about him. I'm pretty sure he's absolutely in the clear."

I took a train to Leicester Square and walked through to the Chichester Hotel. I didn't go in for a minute or two, for I was wondering if the risk was worth while. Then as I moved to cross the road I saw someone emerge from the hotel doors, and the hall porter was with him, carrying a largish bag. The light was good and I knew the man was Martin Collier.

The porter whistled and almost at once a taxi drew up. A second or two and it moved off, and just as I stepped forward to get its number a car came by and I had to dodge back quickly to avoid it. And by then the taxi had rounded the corner into Coote Street.

I went into the hotel and flashed my card at the desk. It was a quiet, first-class hotel and the clerk rather raised his eyebrows. I explained about a hotel swindler we were looking for and together we had a look at the book. When I left a minute or two later I knew that Martin Collier had stayed at that hotel the previous night. And the Chichester was exactly four minutes' sharp walking from the Royalty. I knew because I tried it out.

*

When I got back to the Yard there was a message for me. James Halsing was with Wharton and Matthews, and Wharton wasn't anxious for Halsing to see me, so I wrote a report downstairs about the visit to Lilian Rome's flat.

I added a rider and I could have added two. What I didn't say was that unless there had been any collaboration between Lilian and her nephew—and, frankly, I thought that a pretty fantastic idea—then Lilian could be crossed off as a suspect. After all, it had been a man who had booked Room 323 and lured Posfort there.

What I did say was that something else could be ruled out: the idea that the murderer had to be one who was connected with the literary agency. Everyone who had been anything of a friend of Caroline Halsing, let alone her relations, must have heard from her over and over again the detailed workings of Drench and Posfort. I ended that report with an unwonted touch of optimism. Only twenty-four hours since the enquiry had begun and already we were certain, or so it seemed, of the motive for the murder. Posfort's killing, as I'd be prepared to swear, was a settling of accounts for what he'd done to Caroline Halsing.

Just as I'd finished I was called upstairs. Wharton was sitting back in his desk chair and scowling at what turned out to be a copy of James Halsing's statement.

"You got him here pretty quick," I said to Wharton.

"We ran him down in Town," he told me. "He went back with his brother-in-law, the actor. Have a glance at this."

I gave Matthews a look as I took that statement, but he merely shrugged his shoulders. I soon knew why.

It was at about ten o'clock on that Thursday morning, the statement ran, when the telephone went at Ralehurst Rectory, and James Halsing answered it.

"Is that the Reverend Halsing?"

"Who's speaking, please?"

"It doesn't matter who's speaking. Who're you?"

"I'm his son, James Halsing. Can I take a message?"

There was a slight pause.

"Perhaps you'll do as well, Mr. Halsing. You know what happened to your sister?"

It was Halsing who paused.

"I say, who *are* you?"

"I'm a friend of your sister. You don't know me, but I knew her, and I know all about Posfort. I want to put a proposition up to you."

"What is it?"

"If you feel like landing Posfort in trouble, I can help you. I mean real trouble. Something he'll be very sorry for. Are you game to do it?"

"Depends exactly what it is."

"I'll tell you about that personally. Can you be at the Royalty Hotel at seven-thirty tonight? Room 323. Seven-thirty sharp."

"Yes, I think I can manage it. All the same, I'd rather you told me what it's all about."

"I'll be there myself," the voice said. "If I'm not I'll be downstairs in the main lobby. Look for a shortish man in a brown suit and I'll have a red carnation in my buttonhole. And one very important thing. Not a word to a soul, even your father. Now I come to think of it, I don't think he'd approve."

So James Halsing rode his motor-bike to Orpington and left it in the car-park at the cinema and took a train to Town. At seven-thirty he went to Room 323, but something unusual seemed to be happening, for that was when the photographers were leaving. So he nipped downstairs and looked for the man in the brown suit. He was not there, so he went upstairs again. He was reconnoitring that room when I saw him. And feeling then that something was badly wrong, he nipped downstairs again, had another quick look for the man in the brown suit and then went back to Orpington.

The voice on the telephone, he said, had been that of an educated man, but rather hard to describe. There had been something muffled about it. Asked what he thought the scheme might have been, he said he didn't know, unless the idea had been to catch out Posfort in the hotel room with another woman.

"Well, what d'you make of it?" Wharton said.

"I'm inclined to believe it," I told him. "If he was making up a yarn he'd have thought of something that didn't fit in as well as it does. He didn't know that Posfort was lured to that room, too, by someone calling himself Corland. That's something the newspapers haven't yet got."

"I liked him," Matthews said. "I think everything he told us was true. And that hotel scheme, whatever it was, would have been right up his alley."

"Yes," Wharton said, "but suppose it had been the father who'd answered the telephone. What then?"

"Who knows?" I said. "Probably the voice would have told him it had important information about the daughter. Then old Halsing might have turned up at that room instead of his son."

"The idea being to incriminate one of the family."

That was obviously what had been at the back of the whole thing, to have a ready-made suspect who would divert attention from the real murderer. That muffled disguise of the voice might have meant anything. What it didn't do was prove that the owner of the voice was someone whom James Halsing knew.

"We've got two choices," Wharton said: "to believe the story or disbelieve it. Let's say we believe it, till we can prove otherwise."

"That's the best line, sir," Matthews said. "After all, once he was challenged about that statement to Mr. Travers, he didn't try any more lies. He owned up the alibi was a fake."

"Admitted, but where's it get us?"

Nobody had any ideas, unless it was that the murderer was an even cleverer person than we'd thought.

"Not so clever," Wharton said. "If we believe James Halsing, then he's merely eliminated what might have been a genuine suspect. But let's say this statement is a pack of lies. Where's that get us?"

Obviously, again, the first thing to do was to prove it lies, and how to do that nobody knew. James Halsing had admitted being at the Royalty at seven-thirty and only some fantastic stroke of luck could prove he was there a quarter of an hour before.

"How did you get on?" I asked Matthews.

He'd spent his evening checking at the Royalty and the men there had come across no-one who had seen anyone entering or emerging from Room 323. As we seemed to be getting nowhere, I gave an account of my own evening. Wharton didn't seem at all excited about Martin Collier and his refusing to give an alibi.

"According to you, he's just a young service officer, like that young Halsing. You're not telling me that either had the brains to carry out that murder?"

"But why wouldn't he give an alibi?" Matthews wanted to know.

Wharton looked at his watch.

"Ten o'clock. A bit late now, but you slip round in the morning and see if he had a young lady in tow. And you might get something from the hall porter about where he went to in that taxi. If not, his aunt might know where he is."

My instructions were to look into the alibis of the Haze brothers. Bridget Halsing would probably not be properly awake, I said, till the afternoon, so I'd run down to Marland in the morning and check Roland Haze's alibi first. Wharton, I thought, wasn't looking too happy. He said he too had had a dud day, though he mentioned only a call on Posfort's solicitors and a finding out that there had been no will. Not that a will would have helped, as he said. Money wasn't a motive, or else his name was Robinson.

As I walked home I couldn't get out of my head that idea of collaboration. By the time I was at the flat, the trickles of thought were a stream. Everything, I could tell myself, pointed to at least a couple of hands and brains in that murder scheme, even if one, hand alone had held the gun. And however much Wharton had sneered at it, you couldn't altogether discard the evidence of that chambermaid. Wharton might shut his ears to that evidence, but that was far from proving it unreliable. As I saw things, the tragedy of Caroline Halsing affected her whole family and her friends. That the father had been stunned into a kind of indifference was far from a proof that others concerned had been content to let Posfort not only get away with responsibility for her death but be left free to play fast and loose with a new woman.

What disheartened me, as it was probably disheartening Wharton, was the knowledge that collaboration would make that murder one that could never be solved. All A. had to do was to swear to the alibi of B. and that would be the end of it. That was why I lay so long awake, with every possible combination of A. & B. running through my mind. Maybe it was the very monotony of it all that finally sent me to sleep.

When I woke in the morning I was still convinced that I was right. And though I had no need of confirmation that the murderer was a friend or relation, I saw even more clearly how the actual killing fitted so snugly in: that blasting of holes in Posfort's belly and the agonising death that had followed.

"You tortured Caroline Halsing, now see how you like this!"

That was what the murderer had virtually said, and if I had not been doing the job I was I could have found in my heart some sneaking sympathy. As it was, I had an alibi to check, though when I had got my car at the garage I didn't make for Westminster Bridge. I had rung Norris the previous day at the Agency and I thought I'd better look in at Broad Street.

But everything there turned out to be well in hand. I did have another look at my map. Marland was more to the west than Ralehurst and rather more off the beaten track. I made the two villages about twenty miles apart—not that that mattered. What I decided to do was to take the turn at Lewisham clock and make for the by-pass. If the side roads after that were too tortuous, then I might come home another way.

6

ALIBIS

IT WAS not a good journey. Stream after stream of traffic held me up as far as the by-pass, and then I twice went wrong in country lanes. It was eleven o'clock when I got to the village of Marland. Far out as it was, it had not wholly escaped suburbia, maybe because it was a railway junction. I had to go through quite a long avenue of bungalows before I got to the village itself. Even as scenery it turned out to be worth the while, for it was as pretty a village as I'd seen in a long time. It had quite a spacious green, round which were one or two large houses among the cottages. Facing it, too, was the general store, and a tiny lane led off to the church, no more than a hundred yards away. Next door to the store was what looked like quite a good pub, the Fox and Geese.

It might be as well, I thought, to see where Haze actually lived, and I was told to go straight on for a couple of hundred yards and take a fork to the left and it would be the last house before the railway station. I would have called it a cottage rather than a house, and remarkably presentable it was. Its roof was thatched and a side garage had been skilfully built on. There was a garden at the front with the usual crazy paving path and what seemed a much larger garden at the back. The cottage itself looked as if it might have two small rooms at the front and a kitchen at the back and maybe three bedrooms. The whole place was in a beautiful state of repair.

The railway station was no eyesore. I went on down the hill to reverse my car and I wouldn't have known it was there if I hadn't seen the level-crossing at the bend. Soon after I'd turned the car round I overtook what looked like a railway porter coming off duty. I drew the car alongside him.

"Which is Mr. Haze's house?"

"On the right, just ahead of you," he told me. "But you won't find him at home. He was on the eight fifty-five this morning."

"He lives there alone?"

"He does now," he said. "Ever since his mother died. That was a year and more ago. Now he has someone to look after him."

I asked if I could give him a lift, but he said he had only a few yards to go. I drove on to the green and parked the car just short of the pub. A bell tinkled above the door of the little shop as I went in. The smell of paraffin, cheese and leather took me nostalgically back to the Suffolk village of my boyhood. I was smiling to myself as a pleasant-faced woman came in from the back.

"I wonder if you could help me," I said. "I went to see Mr. Haze, but he doesn't seem to be at home. I called on him on Thursday evening, but he wasn't at home then, either."

"He goes to Town every day," she told me. "But you wouldn't have found him on Thursday night because he was at the concert. Got up by the British Legion, it was."

"You saw him there?"

"He sat right next to me."

"What time was that?"

"About seven," she said. "He came in just as it started and he sat next to me the whole while."

"Then I probably just missed him," I said. "He'll be home this afternoon?"

"Bound to be," she said. "Far as I know he always comes home about dinner-time Saturdays. Most of the gentlemen round here do."

"Then no doubt I'll see him later. I have to go to the rectory in any case. It's by the church, isn't it?"

By the church it was. I went along the narrow lane, past the village hall, and there, practically on the church-yard, was a Georgian house, almost the spit of the one at Ralehurst. I went on to the church first. A notice told me that the incumbent was the Rev. Donald Troop, M.A. (Cantab.). I opened the door and looked in, and I came almost face to face with the rector himself. He was a man of my own age; shortish, almost pot-bellied, and with a round, rubicund face.

"Come in, my dear sir," he told me heartily. "You were about to look round our church?"

I know nothing about ecclesiastical architecture and I certainly did not want a conducted tour.

"As a matter of fact I was hoping to find somebody," I said, and stepped back to the porch. "I wanted some information. By the way, I see you're a Cambridge man."

It's a tricky job checking an alibi if you're not to embarrass the person concerned. The woman at the shop had been easy, but she was of a different social class. Already Troop was giving me a suspicious look. Maybe he thought I was some new kind of trickster trying to make a touch.

"We look about the same age," I went on. "Maybe we were contemporaries."

It turned out that we had been, though he was a Pembroke man and I'd been at Downing. At any rate, almost before we knew it, we were walking along the path, back in the days that were no more. At the rectory porch he asked me in for a sherry.

"Very good of you," I said, "but I have to get back to Town. I'd really come to see a Mr. Haze, but he isn't in. Do you know him?"

"Very well indeed," he said. "He and I happen to be members of a local bridge four. A very charming fellow."

Then he was frowning.

"I happened to see him this morning by the station. We've had a most terrible happening here. One of our best known parishioners was struck down last night and robbed. I'd been up to his house for a word with his widow."

"He was killed?"

"Unhappily, yes. A terrible affair. I only hope the police catch the one who did it."

"Yes," I said. "One doesn't expect things like that in a quiet little village like this."

I managed to mention a fruitless call at Haze's cottage on the Thursday night.

"He wasn't in," Troop said. "He was at the village hall. There was a concert party in aid of our British Legion. He gave me a press cutting he'd promised me. About Burma. I spent a few years there before the war."

"Before or after the show?"

"Just after it'd begun," he said. "Just after one of the opening sketches, as far as I remember. I do know he had to go home just before the interval." He gave a chuckle. "He'd forgotten and left something on the stove. I thought women were the ones who did that."

"Well, I'll be getting back to Town," I said, and held out my hand. "I'll give Haze a ring this afternoon."

So that was very definitely that. Roland Haze was indisputably in the clear. In a minute or two I was on the road again, and this time I was aiming to come into the main road well below Bromley. Not far short of it I came to an hotel that looked as if it might supply a meal, so I drew the car up. Then I saw the notice advertising lunches. I was told the meal would be on at twelve-thirty, so I had a drink in the bar to fill in time.

It was quite a good meal, and over coffee in the small lounge I had a look at the latest of a stack of cheap illustrated weeklies. An advertisement caught my eye. It was the kind of thing I'd seen somewhere before: two photographs side by side, and in big letters above them:

WHICH IS THE REAL THING?

I've more than an allergy to quite a lot of modern pictorial advertising: the kind that takes a mustard-seed of possible truth and produces from it a monstrous tree. Take Bunko and soon you'll be sitting in the boss's chair. A cupful of Bunko regularly and you too may climb Everest. That kind of thing. People with balloons issuing from their mouths. "Thinks—if only I could induce him to take Vito!"

I wouldn't have given that advertisement a second look if the two photographs hadn't been of Churchill, and I'd wondered what need there had been for two photographs side by side. Then I saw what it was all about. Only one photograph was the real thing—that on the right. The one on the left was of a Mr. X. of So-and-So.

My eye went on and then came back. The rest of the advertisement hadn't interested me. What had caught my eye was a word at the very foot—VARGO. That advertisement, it appeared, had been to emphasise that, whatever other jams or marmalades might be, Vargo's was THE REAL THING, BREKFAST marmalade and BREKFAST jams, made by Vargo Products Limited, Hanford, S.W.16.

Roland Haze had an important job with Vargo Products Limited, so Martin Collier had said. As I remembered that, I remembered something else; where I had seen a similar kind of advertisement. Something arose out of it that made me wonder if I could put it to Haze himself, just to satisfy my curiosity. I smiled to myself. Of course I could ring Haze. If he were home it would be only courtesy to let him know about his alibi. So I rang him and he was in.

"Travers here, Mr. Haze. I thought you'd like to know that alibi of yours was all in order."

"Very good of you," he said. "Not that I was very worried."

"By the way, I just saw an advertisement of your firm. The one with two pictures of Churchill. Aren't you people afraid of an action for breach of copyright?"

"How do you mean?"

"Well, there used to be advertisements of the same kind by some firm who advertised extensively in the American *Saturday Evening Post*."

"I don't think you need worry," he told me. "If we'd been out of order we'd have heard about it long ago."

"Well, if you get in trouble I'll bail you out," I said, and he gave his quiet laugh.

I rang Bridget Halsing from a police station just short of Town and she said she would be available in a quarter of an hour's time. Her block of flats simply reeked of money. The room in which we talked might have been the drawing-room of a fine old Queen Anne house.

You couldn't call her beautiful, but her face had character and vivacity. She was more mature than her sister, but there was a strong likeness all the same.

"You've met my husband," she said, and Courtney Haze waved a hand at me from across the room. He brought the cigarette box.

"Or don't you smoke when on duty?"

"Don't be horrid," his wife said. "Besides, it's only that they don't drink—" She broke off with a look of alarm.

"Did you notice that I was calling you *they*?"

"Why not?" I told her amusedly. "The law's supposed to be impersonal. *They*, as my old nurse used to tell me, are the cat's children."

"Something in that," Courtney said. "There's a logic in it, if I could only see where."

"Let's sit down and get this horrible business over," she said, so we sat down. Courtney placed an ash-tray at my elbow, then settled himself with crossed legs in an easy chair. The look in his eyes, it seemed to me, was rather ironic.

I started to explain about the need for an alibi. Bridget sat frowning, as if it were all so hard to understand.

"What you want to know is where Courtney was at seven o'clock that night," she said. "I can tell you. He was sitting right under my nose in the second row of stalls. I was furious with him. He hadn't said a word about being there and he knows I simply hate being startled like that. I always go, if I can, to the first night of any show of his and then I keep away."

"You married, Mr. Travers?" he asked quietly.

"Now, darling, you're being horrid again. What he's trying to tell you, Mr. Travers, is that I'm different from any other woman."

"So you are, darling, or I'd never have married you." She smiled at him. They might almost have been coming apart after an embrace.

"All the same," she told me, "I almost wish it had been my husband who'd killed that swine of a man."

"Provided they didn't hang me."

"Of course they wouldn't have hanged you, not if they'd known the truth."

I was feeling the tiniest bit uncomfortable. It was almost as if I was a shuttlecock being flicked from one to the other.

"Well, I'm obliged to you both," I told them, "but there's one thing I have to point out. Your evidence, Mr. Haze, is supported solely by your wife. You surely know that has no validity in law? Who else can swear you were where you were on Thursday night?"

"Yes," he said. "Perhaps I should have thought of that. To tell you the truth, we were rather hoping to—" He broke off. The grin was rueful. "Sorry, but I didn't mean to tell you that."

"Let me guess at it," I said. "You talked it over and knew you had only your wife's word, and you reckoned that might be good enough."

"That's roughly it. What I can add is that I rang Tom Usher, the stage manager, on the Thursday morning and mentioned a stall, and he told me he'd try to fix it. When I arrived a seat was waiting for me at the box office."

"What time was that?"

"Oh, about ten minutes before the curtain went up."

"You spoke to your neighbours?"

"Good lord, no! I was incognito, so to speak. If I'd been spotted, they'd have been talking to *me*. That's why I didn't come in till the curtain was actually going up."

"And where did you sit in the row?"

"The last seat but one. There was just a youngish-looking chap between me and the side exit."

I closed my notebook. That seemed to be all, except that there would have to be formal statements.

"Sorry I've had to bother you," I told them.

"It wasn't a bother," she told me, and I thought she seemed considerably relieved. "Sorry it's too late for coffee and too early for tea. What about a drink now it's no longer official?"

"Afraid it's just the wrong time," I said. "By the way, shouldn't you have been at a matinée?"

"No," she said. "Every other Saturday I take a holiday."

"Bridget has a really brilliant understudy," Courtney cut in. "Besides, you can always pack them in on a Saturday matinée. You've seen the show?"

I said that my wife and I had seen it together, and we'd thought Bridget Halsing had been brilliant. No wonder the play was having a long run.

"By the way," I added quickly, "I might tell you, strictly between ourselves, that I've been to Marland this morning. Your brother's alibi is all right and tight."

"Good," he said. "Not that I had any qualms."

"Roland's a darling," Bridget told me earnestly, without a trace of gush. "Very quiet and rather shy, but an absolute darling. So dependable."

"Afraid we didn't put up a very good show for you yesterday," Courtney said. "We were all just a bit on edge. We've all had to be a bit like ostriches, hiding our heads in the sand. I mean about that dreadful business. Your coming along brought everything a bit too close again."

"Just one of those things that had to be done," I said. "But tell me something. What actually happened between you and Posfort that day when you saw him at his office?"

"He just lied like hell. Swore blind he had nothing to do with it. Tried to throw suspicion on Miss Rome's nephew. And on my brother."

That was about all. As I drove slowly towards the Yard I couldn't help wondering a whole lot of things. I'd just been in the company of two of the most brilliant people in their own profession whom you could probably find in the whole country, and I somehow couldn't get away from the idea that I'd been only a spectator at a short matinée of their own devising. Maybe the two had been acting a comedy: a grim comedy, even if the touches had been so light and somehow so sure. Maybe that alibi wasn't worth the breath that had given it. I even thought that maybe the husband and wife might after all be the wanted A. and B.

Wharton was in: the debris of a tea-tray in front of him. He pushed it away as I came in. He didn't look happy about the comparatively negative results of my day.

"We ought to be able to get something from that stage manager," he said. "It's just possible we might be able to learn who occupied the seats each side of him"—it was Courtney Haze he meant. "I think I'll drift round there myself. I might even see the show. Not a bad idea to know the sort of people you're dealing with."

"Matthews get anything?"

"At the Chichester? Not a lot. Young Collier's at Portsmouth, though. Matthews has gone down there. If Collier doesn't talk, Matthews will bring him back."

At the moment there was nothing for me to do. If there was anything from Matthews, then George would let me know in the morning—a Sunday morning, when enquiries might be difficult to make. The sight of the *Financial Times* among the papers on the side table reminded me of something. I looked up Vargo Products Limited and found there had been dealings. Their five shilling shares were quoted at six and threepence. I found the *Stock Exchange Annual* among the reference books in the case and looked at it too. Between it and Haley's comprehensive *Limited Liability Companies* I got what I wanted, though that was merely the satisfying of a curiosity about the name Vargo. The firm of R.W. Varley of Tonbridge, jam makers, had been bought up by Goring and Haze of London, and the new company had also amalgamated the names. Roland Haze was a director, which explained why Martin Collier had thought him older than he was.

Haze I had put at about thirty-six, and if he were as shy and reserved as Bridget Halsing had told me, then there had probably been a certain amount of nepotism about that directorship. I also realised that the firm's factory and registered offices were nearer Catford than Lewisham, and that I might actually have passed them that morning on the homeward journey without noticing the name. That would be handy for Haze's cottage at Marland: twenty minutes or so in the train from Marland Junction. Not that any of it mattered, as I told Wharton when he asked me what I was looking up.

I went home to a quiet evening at the flat. After a service dinner I went on with *The Flying Beacon*, a copy of which I'd bought at Charing Cross Station. It was a fine book, and I was quite startled when the telephone went and I saw it was well after ten o'clock.

"Wharton here. You might like to know that our young friend has talked. Just what I thought. A lady friend spent the night at the same hotel."

"Thought he was heartbroken about the other one."

"He said this was a kind of rebound. Nothing to it at all. No alibi, though. He and this girl didn't dare have meals together. They met at a restaurant just off Sloane Square—the Pied Peacock—at seven-thirty. Plenty of taxis always at the Royalty. He could have got from there to Sloane Square in ten minutes."

"He'd have had to be lucky," I said. "What're you going to do? Check up on taxis?"

He said resignedly that that was what it would come to. He didn't cheer up when I asked him about the show. He said he'd seen better in his time.

George doesn't care for comedies of manners. The homely and sentimental is more in his line: you could even imagine him at *East Lynne*, wiping away a furtive tear. I put away my book and went to bed, and I was anticipating the comforting warmth and a quiet thinking about my afternoon. I did begin thinking, and about Courtney Haze and how young he had looked that afternoon. There had been something almost boyish about him as he had sat in that chair, legs crossed, and that ironic—almost impish—smile on his unlined face. But I didn't get as far as A. and B. In the middle of the same thought, it must have been, I fell asleep.

And there—I hope in some ways it will be a shock to you—ended the Posfort Case, at least as far as concerned myself. Not that I didn't continue to do things. We all did things until there was no more to do than try the old things all over again. On the Thursday night, exactly a week after the killing of Posfort, I ceased to be on the paid list. I suppose I could have footled on, but I had no heart in it. All I had was a gnawing curiosity. Maddening is perhaps the better word, especially when I began to realise that something had happened to which I should never have an answer.

What would you have done? Or would you rather hear what we did and then point out the omissions? If the latter, then this is a brief but comprehensive account. From first to last a good number of men were employed on it.

Enquiries were going on all the time at the Royalty. People who had left it were questioned with the co-operation of provincial police forces, and out of all that one thing only emerged. A man who had been immediately behind the pseudo-Corland at the desk gave something of a description of him. As near as could be assessed he was about five feet nine, had hair slightly greying at the temples, wore horn-rimmed glasses, had a moustache and carried a fibre case. It was the case that made the informant notice him, for it had been put down near him and he had tripped over it and almost fallen. The pseudo-Corland had muttered an apology.

Important though that seemed, it was worth little. Had the informant noticed any bodily peculiarity, or the shape of the ears and the colour of the eyes, it would have been different. Height can be increased by heels or insoles: hair can be whitened at the temples and a false moustache, if put on with care, could not be detected in artificial light. Make-up, skilfully applied, can change the complexion, and darkening under the eyes can give an appearance of age. All that was of interest was that the murderer had made himself as much like the Corland of the book jacket as possible, even to the hair, for in that photograph the play of light had given it an appearance of greying at the temples.

Martin Collier's flimsy alibi was given special attention. The girl had been out in the late afternoon, paying a call that would help to explain her staying for the night in Town, and she had gone direct to the little restaurant, chosen, by the way, because she had known it from a meal there with an uncle. It was all part of her elaborate alibi.

Collier said he had gone by Underground and had left the hotel at about seven o'clock, but that could not be proved. On the other hand, no taxi could be found that had taken him shortly after a quarter past seven from the Royalty or near it to Sloane Square or near it.

As for the gun, Collier had seen service in the Mediterranean and might have acquired it there. So too might any man who had seen service in Italy during the war. That Italian 6.35 mm.

was the sort of thing that could be put into a woman's hand-bag, and yet a woman couldn't have done the killing—unless she had had an accomplice who did the registration for Room 323. As to enquiries about the gun, every gun-smith in Town had been questioned about the sale of one, and pawnshops had been circularised too.

The telephone call which James Halsing said had brought him to the Royalty that night had not been traced. Every other detail of his story was correct, including the time of taking his motor-bike from the cinema car-park. He had seen the programme that afternoon purely, he now said, to pass the time before going to the Royalty.

Wharton spread the net even wider. Since nothing seemed to be emerging that would incriminate Caroline Halsing's relatives or intimate friends, he tackled Lilian Rome about disgruntled clients. All she could do was provide him with three who had left the agency in the course of the preceding year. I understood they were questioned, and if each had not had an excellent alibi I should have heard of it. After that Wharton wanted a list of the firm's clients and a list of all publishers, English and foreign, with whom the firm had had dealings. Lilian told him stoutly that the whole thing was preposterous, and that if business was lost by such grossly unwarranted interference, then she'd certainly bring an action. That worried Wharton about as much as a hiccough. Lilian had to provide that list, though what came of it I never learned. I rather think Wharton began to realise just how intricate that kind of investigation was.

As to Courtney Haze, enquiry at booking agencies and else-where failed to produce that youngish man who had sat on the far side of him. An appeal had been made in the Press and no-one had come forward, but the couple were found who had sat on the other side of Haze. They were a newly-engaged couple, more interested in themselves than their neighbours, but they did say that Haze had taken his seat just as the curtain was rising and that he had gone out just before the only interval. Asked about the youngish man who had been on the other side of Haze, they said they hadn't really noticed him. He too had gone out during the interval.

As for what I did myself, that included another visit to Ralehurst. What I wanted was a closer observation of the Rev. Timothy Halsing, but all I had was a highly disconcerting experience. What happened was this.

I didn't want to arrive in the morning in case Halsing should be busy on parochial work, so I tried to catch him not long after lunch. The same maid showed me into the study and went to tell Halsing I was there. I waited less than a minute before he came in. In the second or two before he spoke I couldn't help seeing how ill he looked. His face was thinner and pale and his eyes were like black pits in the bony skull. There was something distraught about his manner and the whirlwind way he had come in.

"Yes?" he demanded, and the voice was almost shrill. "What is it you want?"

I was so taken aback I couldn't find words.

"If you've come about my daughter—get out!"

"Just a moment, Mr. Halsing—"

"Get out!"

He was glaring so menacingly that I took him at his word.

"I'm sorry you choose to take this extraordinary attitude," I told him as I went past him to the door. "Perhaps later you may think better of it."

I could feel his eyes on my back as I crossed the hall. As I let myself out he was still watching me from the study door.

I don't think Wharton quite believed me when I reported it; in retrospect I hardly believed it myself.

"What was the matter with him? Suddenly gone balmy or something?"

"He was certainly in a highly nervous condition," I said. "Maybe he'd decided after my last visit not to like me. Or he might have had a guilty conscience."

I rather gathered that Wharton made some enquiries through the local police, but if anything had emerged to make Halsing a suspect, I'm pretty sure he'd have told me. But about the rest of that afternoon. I had so much time on my hands that I thought I'd go round by Marland, more to pass the time than anything else, for I knew that Roland Haze would not be at home. But he was. At least I came in by the station as a train was moving out, and when the gates were opened I overtook him. He got in beside me, and when we'd done the couple of hundred yards to his cottage he asked me to have some tea. I said I'd be very glad to.

Things had been rather slack at his office, he said, and he'd come home early, and it was one of his bridge nights too. While we were having tea I told him about my visit to Halsing. He said he wasn't surprised. He'd heard a whisper from his brother that Halsing had been acting peculiarly. It had all arisen out of the tremendous shock of Caroline's death.

I was in no hurry after the tea and he seemed pleased to have company, so we sat on talking. I must say I found him the friendly, rather quiet but extremely likeable fellow that both his rector and his sister-in-law and even Martin Collier had described. His age, by the way, was exactly the thirty-six that I'd guessed, but as he sat quietly talking there by the fire he looked much older. It was chiefly about Spain that he talked. His firm had certain orange interests there and he told me he might be going there himself for a week or two in the very immediate future.

I thought about him from time to time as I was driving home and perhaps because I wanted to keep old Halsing from my mind. Martin Collier had described Haze as stuffy: I thought how perfectly he was cut out for life in a village, and, for that matter, for the life of a bachelor. That younger passion of his for Caroline Halsing, I told myself, had been very much of an aberration. Maybe there had been more than a philosophical calm in his acceptance of her preference for those who, like Martin Collier, were more of her age.

Collier, by the way, was at sea again, in a light cruiser bound for Singapore. He, like myself, was definitely out of the Posfort Case.

7

THE MARLAND AFFAIR

I WAS reading my newspaper on the Saturday morning and wondering with all the illogic in the world if I should see anything about the Posfort Case. It was not only illogical as a hope but also ridiculous, for if there'd been any new developments Wharton would surely have rung me. Besides, as far as I knew the Press had now been told everything.

They even knew about the hotel registration in the name of Humbert Corland. Corland, I had thought, had had some fine publicity.

At any rate I was looking through that paper with such care that I noticed the word Marland. It said that Scotland Yard was being called in abut the Rickson murder and it gave a very brief re-hash. Rickson had been found on the evening of the 11th of November on a path that led to his house. A blow on the head had killed him and he had been robbed. His attaché case and wallet had both gone. He was said to be a member of a firm of accountants.

Long before I'd finished reading, I knew that the murder was the one that Troop, the Marland rector, had told me about on that Saturday morning when I'd been enquiring into Roland Haze's alibi. I had a feeling of uneasiness. Wharton always liked to be told every single detail about an enquiry, and I hadn't mentioned that murder in my report. There was no reason why I should. A robbery with violence, even if it happened in Marland, had nothing to do with the Posfort Case. All the same, something was telling me to keep my mouth shut. What the eye doesn't see the heart doesn't grieve for. Wharton still needn't be told that I'd ever heard of that Marland murder.

A few minutes later I was beginning to wonder. If Wharton knew that the Yard was being called in, and therefore knew about that murder, mightn't he attach an undue importance to the fact that it had been committed in Marland? Something was urging me to find out. I could ring him and pretend myself to be surprised at what was, after all, a coincidence. Or would it be better to do nothing? Then curiosity, as ever, got the better of me, and I did ring him. He was out, and so was Matthews. I felt relieved. Half an hour later, just as I was thinking of drifting along to Broad Street, Wharton rang me. That calling in of the Yard hadn't come to his attention, but he too had noticed the Marland coincidence—if one could call it that—and had got hold of the local Chief Constable.

"Naturally I didn't tell him we'd once had a Posfort Case suspect at Marland, but he said he'd referred to us because he'd like our help at the London end. The firm of accountants the dead man worked for is—wait a minute—is Ampleton, Hughes and Co. of Savenhall Street."

"What can you do at this end?"

"The attaché case. Why was that taken?"

"On the off-chance there was something valuable in it."

"Why shouldn't there have been some documents that incriminated someone or other in fraud or something of the sort? That is what's been put up to us."

I had to chuckle.

"Keep that for the Marines, George. The horse variety. You're hoping for something to fit in with quite a different case."

"And I mightn't be so far wrong at that," he told me. "At any rate I said I'd have a look round at the spot, just as a preliminary. His inspector's meeting me there. If you'd like to be here—purely unofficially—in a few minutes, you could go down with me."

It was as good a way of spending the morning as any, so I once more went to Marland. Rickson's house—Whiteways—lay on the far side of the station. When you're driving a car you see little of what's around you and I was surprised to see—it was something I'd missed on my first visit—that beyond the station there were quite a few biggish houses. Marland, in fact, was a much larger place than I'd thought. I ought to have known otherwise. A place so handy for Town was bound to have quite a few city or retired men among its population.

An Inspector Kale was waiting for us to show the lie of the land. The station was in a slight valley. Woods—chestnut principally—lay beyond it, and it was in the wood clearings that those better-class houses stood. Two separate ways led to Rickson's house. From the main lane was a thirty-yard approach to house and garage. Well short of it, and making a very tapering triangle with lane and approach, was a path beginning at the lane and leading through a few youngish trees and their scanty undergrowth to Rickson's front gate. It was about half-way along that path that he had been struck down and killed.

The area, Kale told us, had been cordoned off at once and he had had a couple of men searching the neighbourhood of the path. Nothing in the way of a clue had been found.

"No weapon found yet?" Wharton asked him.

Nothing whatever had been found. The weather had been fine for a few days and that path was hard and there hadn't even been a footprint.

"Any burglaries round here?"

"Three in the autumn, all the same night," the inspector said. "We never got him."

"And what's your idea about this?"

The inspector shrugged his shoulders.

"Your idea, sir, is probably as good as mine. I'd say some cosh merchant or someone of the kind hanging about and happening to see Mr. Rickson."

"A long way from home, wasn't he?" Wharton asked dryly.

"They're all over the place, sir. Might have been someone looking round on the chance of another burglary."

"What was the wound like?"

"Caved the back of his skull in."

"Not much of the cosh about that," Wharton said. "Sounds to me more like a spanner or a length of piping." He grunted. "A cold-blooded customer, whoever he was. He couldn't have taken the wallet till Rickson was dead. Personally, I don't care a lot for that—do you?"

"I'd say he didn't know he was dead, sir. Down Rickson went and he grabbed the wallet and the case, and that was that."

"Maybe. Where's the actual spot?"

Faint traces remained of where the body had been outlined in the hard clay. Rickson had fallen forward. Near his feet was the one tree of any size—a scrub oak. A man could have hidden behind it.

"No street lighting here," Wharton said. "What sort of a night was it?"

"Quite clear, sir. No mist or anything. The moon was almost up, so Mr. Lord says. All the same, it'd have been dark in here."

"Who's he? That Mr. Lord?"

"The man at the next house, about fifty yards down, sir. He and Mr. Rickson were on the six-thirty-five and they walked from the station together."

"No-one else on it?"

"No, sir: not of what you might call the gentry. Most of them come off the six-ten. Some even come on the five-forty. Mr. Rickson happened to have been working late. He doesn't go in on a Saturday morning."

"How old a man was he?"

"Fifty-six, sir. Married and one son. He's now in Kenya. Like to see the photographs of the body, sir?"

"No, no, no. I'll take your word for what happened to his skull."

"Very thin-skulled he was, sir—so we're told."

"You mean that whoever struck him needn't necessarily have meant to kill him?"

"He wouldn't have thought that in any case," I ventured to point out. "He just struck the one blow. If he'd been wanting to be certain he'd killed, then he'd have struck again."

"Something in that," he said. He pursed out his lips and reared himself up for a look around him.

"How did he happen to be found?" I asked.

"Well, sir, Mrs. Rickson expected him on the six-thirty-five. He'd rung in the afternoon to say he might be on it. When he didn't come, she rang Mrs. Lord on the off-chance and Mr. Lord said he'd left him only a minute or two before. So she came out to the front gate to see what'd happened to him and the dog—a cairn—was with her and he started barking and running down the path and then barking away. And that's how she found him. She thought at first he was ill, so she ran and got Mr. Lord and he brought a torch. When he saw what had happened he rang the police."

"Clear enough," Wharton said. "Anyone you'd like me to see?"

The inspector didn't think so. Everyone possible had already been seen. He'd told everything he knew, and what he'd hoped for were suggestions from Wharton. Wharton hadn't any, except possible enquiries in Town.

"What sort of a man was Rickson?"

There was no special reason why I should ask the question: it was more like a filling-in of a gap while Wharton decided whether to go or stay.

"Well, he was pretty well off," the inspector said. "Must be, or he couldn't keep up that place of his, tennis court and all. He was a great man in the local British Legion, they tell me. He was a major or something in the last war."

Wharton held out his hand. The inspector looked a bit surprised.

"Doesn't look as if we can do any more good here. I'll get in touch with your Chief. You might give us a ring yourself if anything turns up."

We went back to our car. I asked if he had any ideas.

"Don't think so," he said. "Looks as if someone on the prowl thought he might be worth the slugging. I can't see any more in it than that."

I agreed. Now we'd seen things, it seemed fantastic that some person who stood in fear of Rickson's accounting should have followed him and killed him for the purpose of destroying evidence that had been in the attaché case. What Rickson had been carrying couldn't have been the sum total of evidence. If I knew anything about accounting, and I did know quite a deal, then even if every document had been destroyed, a case could easily be built up again from the original data on which Rickson had worked.

We had come in by a side road at the station. Wharton was suggesting that we should go to the Fox and Geese and telephone from there. I moved the car on up the slope. As I neared the Haze cottage I saw a man filling a barrow at the gate. There was a heap of ballast and a big mortarboard.

"Haze might be in," I said. "Like to see him if he is?"

"Might as well," he said, so I drew the car in at the verge. We got out.

"Mr. Haze in?" I asked the man. He looked like a jobbing labourer.

"Yes, sir, he's on the back lawn."

"What're you doing?" Wharton asked.

"Making up the crazy path at the back, sir. You have to do these jobs while there's no frost about."

"What do you mean—making up?"

The late Mrs. Haze, it seemed, had had the paths laid and she wouldn't have them cemented in. She liked little Alpine plants to grow in the crevices.

"The trouble was, sir, she forgot about weeds. The whole path got smothered with them, so Mr. Haze had this front path done last spring and now we're tackling the one at the back."

Wharton motioned me ahead and we went round the house to the back. Haze, in an old suit and a British warm over it, was on his hands and knees, laying out the pieces of paving ready for the concrete. His mouth gaped at the sight of me.

"Morning, Haze. You look busy. This is Chief-Superintendent Wharton, by the way. We've been looking into that business of Rickson. You must have heard all about it long ago."

"Well, yes," he said quietly. "In a place like this everybody knows everything."

"Sometimes before it's happened," suggested Wharton, and held out a hand.

Haze was rubbing his hands on his old flannel trousers.

"Afraid I'm a bit dirty," he told us ruefully.

"An honest man's the noblest work of God," Wharton told him, and no wonder Haze gave him a quick look of surprise.

It was a smallish lawn with quite a large oak giving it shade. The path led from the back door to a summer-house that backed on a hedge by the oak.

"You're making a good job of it," I said, for he was laying the path in about three inches of concrete and then filling in the interstices. "No weeds will ever find their way through that."

"This unfortunate man Rickson," Wharton said. "You knew him?"

"I suppose I knew him as well as anyone," Haze said in his quiet way. "Everyone here knows everyone else. Would you like to come to the house? I always have some coffee about this time. Charlie knows how to carry on."

"Well, that's very good of you," Wharton said. "I don't know about coffee, but I'd certainly appreciate the use of your telephone."

To avoid the newly concreted path we went across the grass to a nice little modern kitchen and through it to a hall-passage that separated the two front rooms. The telephone was there. Haze called up the stairs to the invisible woman and asked for three coffees in the lounge. We left Wharton and went into the lounge by the door on the right. I'd been in it before, and as Haze stirred the fire I thought again what a comfortable room it was.

"Cigarette?" Haze said, and offered a box.

He said he preferred a pipe, but he'd have it after the coffee. We sat down and Wharton's voice was coming faintly through the door. I said he'd be wanting information about Rickson, if Haze could provide any. Not that he and I had really been called in to the case.

"When're you going to Spain?"

"On Monday," he said. "I'm flying there. To Seville. It saves an awful lot of time."

Wharton came in. The woman was at his heels with three breakfast cups of coffee and a plate of buns.

"What I call comfort, sir," Wharton said as Haze drew him in a chair. "A nice little place you have here."

"It was my mother's really," Haze told him. "She came here after my father died. He went down in the *Lovenia* during the war. When I came out of the army I moved in with her. It's remarkably handy for the works. Quiet, but I like it."

Wharton took an exploratory pull at the steaming coffee, set his cup hastily down again and helped himself to a bun.

"This Rickson. A very nasty business. What did the village think about it?"

Haze smiled wryly.

"Afraid I'm not conversant with that. Charlie brought the news the next morning. He puts in most Saturday mornings in the garden here. Also, I did see the rector on his way back. I happened to be going to Town that Saturday morning and I met him at the station. He'd been up for a word with Mrs. Rickson. After that I only saw what was in the local paper. Most people seemed to think it was some sort of stray burglar or thief."

"You knew Rickson well?"

"We all know each other well," Haze said mildly. "We usually go up on the same train together. Some of us sometimes manage to get in the same carriages. We run across each other at week-ends. Some of us play bridge together. I don't play golf myself, but some do. There's a nine-hole course at Worfield, about four miles away."

"What sort of a man was Rickson?"

"About the usual run," he said. "A bit overbearing, perhaps. He liked running things. Quite a good chap at heart."

"This job couldn't have been done by someone whose toes he'd trodden on?"

Haze had to smile.

"I don't think so. I admit that he did have a great knack of treading on people's toes, but not to that extent."

Wharton let it drop and switched to the jam and marmalade manufacturing business. Haze's grandfather had founded the parent firm and his own father had been chairman of the amalgamation. It's always interesting to hear an expert talk about something of which you have only a smattering, and Wharton looked quite startled when he glanced at his watch.

"Here we sit talking when we ought to be half-way back to Town. And keeping you from your concreting."

A minute or two later we were on our way.

"A nice, inoffensive sort of chap," Wharton told me, with a nod back at the cottage. "Wouldn't mind a place like his myself, some day."

He was quiet while I overtook a van on the narrow lane.

"Can't say I care a lot for coincidences, though."

"Not much of a coincidence," I told him. "It isn't as though Posfort had been killed at Marland. All it amounts to is that there's been a murder—more of a manslaughter—at Marland, and one of the people possibly concerned with Posfort happens to live there."

"I know, I know," he told me testily. "All the same, I was looking over those reports of yours yesterday afternoon and I told myself that that chap Haze looked the likeliest of the lot—if he hadn't been in the clear. Crippen was an inoffensive sort of chap."

"All right, George," I said. "If you're not satisfied about him, send someone down and turn Marland inside-out. You'll have a fine chance after Monday, when Haze is in Spain."

In the driving mirror I caught his glare.

"Why the devil do you always have to take me so seriously? A man can joke, can't he?"

"Why not?" I said. "Maybe I'm a bit thick in the head, or else your jokes are a bit too abstruse. What did you tell the Chief Constable, by the way?"

"Just that we'd go through the motions of making enquiries at Rickson's firm. You have to be polite to these chaps. You never know if they've got pals among the Big Bugs."

We were out of the lanes and in traffic, and George likes me to keep my mind on the road. It was one o'clock when we got back to the Yard.

"Let me know if anything turns up," I told him. "And thanks for the ride."

Two things turned up. Courtney Haze remembered something else about his alibi: that he had gone out—as we knew—just before the first curtain fell and had had a drink with the stage manager. As George told me, when ringing me up about it, he must have been very ill-at-ease to have thought anything so flimsy worth the reporting.

The other thing that happened arose out of a chance meeting with Matthews a week or two later. I was waiting to cross the road at Trafalgar Square when he got off a bus that drew up at the red light.

"What've you been doing with yourself?" I asked him.

"Keep it under your hat," he said, "but I've had a couple of days at Marland."

"The Rickson case?"

"Yes and no," he said, and: "What about a cup of coffee with me, sir? I've got plenty of time."

It turned out that Wharton had had some kind of hunch about that coincidence he had mentioned to me, and had sent Matthews down to Marland to begin all over again enquiries into Roland Haze.

"Everything was right and tight," Matthews told me. "Nothing new at all. The Old Man must have had some bee in his bonnet."

"No wonder income tax is what it is," I said. "Still, if he's satisfied now, that's all that counts. What about the Rickson business? There's been nothing much in the papers."

"Our end was an absolute wash-out. What he had in that attaché case was just an open and above-board job he was taking home for the weekend, plus a couple of newspapers. His secretary knows because she put the papers in just before he left."

That then was the real end of the Posfort Case. Later I heard that the Yard was still helping on the Rickson Case and the usual chief-inspector and sergeant were still operating round Marland on what had always looked a pretty hopeless enquiry. No weapon had been found; no empty attaché case and no empty wallet. The only evidence, in fact, had been the dead man himself, and he was in Marland churchyard.

Not that either enquiry would ever be shelved. Every document would be meticulously filed, and it would always be someone's responsibility to keep an ear to the ground.

Sooner or later there might be a cross-reference. A man incriminated, for instance, in some other robbery with violence might let out something that connected him with the death of Rickson. The Posfort Case wasn't so hopeful as that, and yet one never knew.

I had ceased to take more than my usual curiosity interest in either, for something had turned up to keep me busy at the Agency. It happened the very morning after I'd met Matthews.

PART II
The Case of Richard Alton

8

A MISSING MAN

I GOT to the Agency at about half-past nine.

"Something this morning I'd like your decision on," Norris said. "It's a bit tricky. To do with that missing schoolmaster."

I had to think for a minute. There was something I faintly remembered, but not much. I'd been too busy over the Posfort Case to pay much attention to anything in the papers except the headlines.

"Wasn't that a week or two back?"

"I looked up some old newspapers at home last night," he said, "and it was just when that Posfort business started. He was working at Queen's School, Dorminster, and had an afternoon off and never came back again. It was reported to the police and apparently they haven't been able to make head nor tail of it, so this young lady—" He broke off. "But you wouldn't know. It started yesterday evening when Metropolitan Enquiries rang us up."

We have close associations with Metropolitan Enquiries. If they're busy and we're slack we sometimes lend them a man or two and they do the same for us. They're a high-class firm, even if they're prepared to handle divorce cases, which we're not.

They'd rung Norris the previous evening and mentioned a Miss Joan Crewe, who'd been to see them about that missing schoolmaster—a Richard Alton. Since the matter was still ostensibly in the hands of the police, they were not prepared to handle it. She had been insistent, however, so they had recommended her to approach us.

"This letter came this morning," Norris said.

It had been written the previous evening from Town and had the address of a women's university club.

Dear Sirs,

I have been recommended by Metropolitan Enquiries Ltd. to see you about an urgent matter and shall be glad if you can see me. Unless I hear from you to the contrary I will call about 2.0 p.m. tomorrow, Tuesday. If you are unable to see me will you telephone me before 11.0 a.m. on receiving this letter. The number is Dorminster 717.

Yours truly,

JOAN CREWE (MISS)

"What do you think, sir?"

I said it looked as if Metropolitan Enquiries were getting rather choosy. If the police had been on the job for best part of three weeks and had got nowhere, there'd be no harm in at least hearing what it was all about.

Dorminster was just about an hour away by train, which was probably why a refusal had to be sent by the time she'd stated. Queen's School, as I knew, was a cathedral foundation and one of the smaller public schools. I looked it up in *The Headmasters' Yearbook*. The school had been re-established in Elizabeth I's time, having been in abeyance after the dissolution of the monasteries—hence its name. It had just under three hundred scholars. The headmaster was a G.M. Scrutt—an Oxford man. There was plenty more, of course, but that was enough.

"Those newspaper cuttings: you've got them here?"

He hadn't. He'd expected me to be far more conversant with the case than I actually was.

"I think I'll put in an hour at the *Record*," I told him. "They keep at least a month's back issues there before sending them to the morgue."

The *Record* is one of the big circulation, popular papers who'd be likely to make a feature of any disappearance that had attached to it any sort of flamboyant mystery. If the Russians were once more sealing off Berlin, you'd find that news on an inside page—if, that is, a film star had just made a fourth marriage. That's what would have the headlines and pictures.

That morning the *Record* didn't let me down. What I learned can be put into one continuous story, for as far as the *Record* was concerned that story didn't break till almost a week after its beginnings. Apparently, however, they had had the news a day or two earlier and had had a smallish paragraph on the middle page. It was just after that, when more news had been released by the police, that banner headlines appeared on the front page.

MISSING SCHOOLMASTER
WAS HE A RED?

But to begin at the beginning. Richard Alton was twenty-eight years old at the time of his disappearance. Shortly after leaving his public school he had done his military service as a lieutenant in an infantry regiment. There was a photograph of him in uniform, which showed him as very good-looking. A description said he was five feet nine, dark-haired, brown-eyed and with a very slight limp—the result of a fall that had broken his ankle.

After his military service he had spent three years at Oxford and had gone almost straight from there to Dorminster, where he taught English and supplementary history to lower and middle forms. He also ran the school dramatic society and was a prominent member of the dramatic society of the city. He seemed to be popular with boys and staff, though some of the latter thought him a bit too assertive in his Socialist views.

On the Wednesday—the day before his disappearance—he spent the evening at rehearsals of *The Cherry Orchard*, which the local dramatic society were shortly putting on. On the Thursday morning at about half-past nine there was a telephone call for him—a distance call, the secretary thought, but one which could not be traced. After it Alton asked a colleague to take a prep. supervision for him as he had to go to Town. He took the three-seventeen, which got him to Town just before half-past four.

That was the last seen or heard of him. The following morning, however, a letter arrived at his rooms—a self-contained flat above a bookseller's shop in Hyde Street, which was only three minutes' walk from the school. It was on plain white paper with no address or date. It had no finger-prints.

> Unless other orders received, report immediately. Bring nothing with you.
>
> P.X.B.

That was the letter. The post-mark was London, W.1. On the Friday, as Alton didn't turn up at the school, a colleague called at the flat and found it locked. On the Saturday morning, with the fear that Alton might have been taken seriously ill during the Thursday night, police assistance was obtained and an entry made. There was no sign of Alton and all his belongings seemed intact, though he had changed from the darkish suit he had worn on the Thursday morning to a brown tweed, a fawn overcoat, brown shoes and a fawn felt hat. There were two private letters and three or four circulars. One of the letters was the cryptic one above and the other from a Miss Joan Crewe (photograph subsequently, but no letter printed).

The police got into touch with Miss Crewe, who was teaching at a select private school for girls—St. Hilda's, Lynham, Dorset. She could throw no light whatever on the matter. In an interview with a representative of the *Record* she agreed that the letter he had received looked as if he had gone to take up some mysterious post. To a suggestion that he might be just another Communist who had been called behind the Iron Curtain, she had seemed to be indignant. Even his Socialism, she said, had been just a phase and not to be taken seriously.

From then on the story ceased to be front-page news, and there were only occasional paragraphs elsewhere. Then it flared up again some time later. Joan Crewe received a letter from Berlin, the British sector. It was completely typewritten. Two things made her certain that it had come from Alton: under the circumstances, no-one else could have sent it, and it also contained a personal allusion.

> Now am I in Berlin, the more fool I. Don't worry about me. Will explain later.
>
> D.

The allusion was to *As You Like It*—Touchstone's *Now am I in Arden*, the more fool I. Joan Crewe had been Celia and Alton Touchstone when that play had been put on a year or two back by the Dorminster Dramatic Society. The D., of course, was Dick. The letter had no fingerprints. The envelope had various ones, but none of them Alton's.

After that there was no reference to the affair in the *Record*. Norris and I lunched together and we both found the whole thing extraordinary. Alton was probably now in East Germany, virtually behind the Iron Curtain, and why he had gone there was altogether beyond us. Assuming that he had been secretly a member of the Party, then why had he been summoned so abruptly? He had not even taken his passport, though doubtless a false one under another name would have been provided by those responsible for sending him to Berlin. But what had he had to contribute to the Cause? What was his value? All the evidence said that he was just a nice young schoolmaster who was happy in his work, popular with practically everybody and with a passion for the theatre. His not too frequent visits to Town had been to indulge in that hobby. As for Communists in a cathedral city like Dorminster, they must have been scarcer than Jews at Berchtesgaden.

Norris is phlegmatic, but I was looking forward with a queer and almost personal interest to the interview with Joan

Crewe. Now and again we're confronted with cases so absorbingly interesting in themselves that I have felt almost a twinge of conscience at taking the money of a client. The disappearance of Richard Alton seemed to me to have all the promise of a case of that kind.

That photograph in the *Record* had been none too good and I scarcely recognised her. To have built her up from the Celia of *As You Like It* would have been just as near, for she was a brunette of about five feet two. Her face was oval and the brown eyes beautifully expressive. It was the face of a person whom one would implicitly trust. Her voice was what I would call modern, but quite charming. I know little about women's clothes in spite of my years of marriage, but I did know, in my limited acquaintance with the jargon, that she was very well dressed: that she was, in fact, what I think is known as *chic*. Even to me the brown ensemble she was wearing was a long way from the ready-made.

Bertha had shown her in and she had given us a quick, quiet look. She smiled as I placed a chair. I said that we had heard from Metropolitan Enquiries, and would probably take the case.

"You're in no hurry, Miss Crewe?"

"You mean this afternoon?"

"Yes, this afternoon. You probably realise that we shall have to do quite a lot of talking."

"My time's entirely my own," she told me. "I do have to get back to Dorminster tonight."

I smiled.

"I don't think you need worry about that. But before you tell us about what you'd like us to do, may I tell you what we've learned already?"

During the ten minutes she didn't once stop me or ask a question. Once or twice she nodded a kind of approval or admission.

"That's all we know at the moment," I said. "Before we ask you to supplement it in any way, will you tell us about yourself?"

"Well, I'm quite able to pay whatever you charge—"

"Not that," I said. "That can come later. Tell us about yourself and Mr. Alton. Help us to build up a background."

She said she was twenty-seven and her twenty-eighth birthday was in two days' time. She had been educated at a private school and had gone on to Girton. After a year at home—her father had had a long illness that was to be fatal—she went to St. Hilda's as a junior geography mistress. Her father—a widower—had been senior partner in a firm of solicitors.

"Would I be right in saying that there's no real need for you to work?"

"Oh, but I like it."

"That's the best of all reasons," I told her. "But about yourself and Mr. Alton."

His parents had been killed in the big blitz of 1942 and he had been looked after by trustees till of age. His father had been rector of St. Jude's, Dorminster. Her own father and the bank had been co-trustees of the Alton estate and she herself had been acquainted with the young Richard Alton long before the local dramatic society had made them friends and colleagues.

"We weren't engaged," she said, "but I think we were both expecting to be."

She had flushed slightly at that.

"It was my fault really. We were practically engaged once, but then we had a quarrel. I thought he was being too attentive to someone else and—well, that was what happened. Then about a year ago we became very friendly again."

Norris leaned forward from the desk.

"Being as unbiased as you can, Miss Crewe, will you tell us just what sort of a young man he was?"

"Well, he was very nice. That's rather trite, but it's the best I can do. Everyone seemed to like him. He was younger, in a way, than I: always rather boyish and full of fun. Very reliable, though—and loyal."

"And this Communist idea. What do you think of it?" Her head shook with a quick anger.

"It's stupid. Utterly stupid! I don't know how anyone could believe anything so preposterous."

"In spite of the fact that he did disappear so suddenly?" I said. "And that he wrote from Berlin?"

"Not in spite of it but because of it," she told me with quite a fierce intensity. "It's not in keeping. How can I explain? I just know that everything's badly wrong. That's why I want you to undertake an enquiry."

"Where did he do his military service?"

"In Germany—after he got his commission."

"He must have made friends there," I said. "Someone among the occupying troops in Germany might be his friend. Even a German there. Did he ever tell you about his experiences in Germany?"

"Well—no. That was before we knew each other sufficiently well. But nothing he's said since was about any particular friends in Germany."

"You'll admit it doesn't rule out the possibility?"

"I think it does. I think he'd have been bound to have said something."

"Let me be frank with you," I said. "If we're not frank with each other, then we might just as well not be here. Let's suppose something: explore an idea that happened to occur to me. Suppose he had been friendly with some woman in Germany and he'd kept in touch with her since. Let's even imagine he'd once been in love with her and she'd appealed for help and he'd gone to Berlin expecting to find her there. Even say the whole thing was purely quixotic."

"Then why didn't he take his passport? Or some clothes?"

"If this woman was actually in East Germany, behind the Iron Curtain, then he'd have had to have secret help. A new passport, a new personality, a new everything. That's why he had to leave so suddenly after being telephoned. He didn't know what he had to do when he got to London. When he did get there and contacted whoever was organising the whole thing, he found out he not only had to leave at once but that everything had to be secret."

She sat there absolutely still, not saying a word. I was about to say something else when she undid her handbag and brought out an envelope. She took a letter from it and held it out to me.

"This is the letter I received from him the morning after he left. Will you read it?"

"The police have seen it?"

"Yes, they made a copy."

It was on pale-blue paper and addressed from his rooms in Hyde Street.

"It's definitely his handwriting?"

"Of course," she said. "There's no possible doubt about it."

I read it slowly, and aloud.

Darling Joan,

How are things with you? About the same, I guess, as they are here. Work gets a bit boring and I occasionally wonder if G.S.—"

"Would that be the headmaster?"

"Yes. He always alluded to him like that. He was very fond of him really."

. . . wonder if G.S. thinks me as good as he once did. Not that I'm very anxious. Rain goes on monotonously most days and that gives one ideas that are apt to be depressing—not that I'm that kind usually. Did you sniff, darling?

Rehearsals are quite good fun and make an exciting break. Don't forget your promise to get here by hook or crook for the first night. Haven't had time to do a lot to my play, but I like what I have done. We'll have a crack at it together. Something's wrong, as I told you, with that first act. It's too mechanical. How and why, I don't know, but that's where you might help. By the way, I had a letter about *News for Grandma* from a variety agent—"

"What's *News for Grandma*? A play?"

"A one-act play. Little more than a sketch, really. He hoped someone would make a variety turn of it. It only lasts about fifteen minutes, but it's very good, and very funny. Too short for the B.B.C. Apparently he thought an agent might get it incorporated in a revue."

I went on reading.

. . . from a variety agent recently. Generally one doesn't expect quick answers from people like that, but there we are, and he seemed to think something could be done with it, which is promising, to say the least of it.

But enough about that, darling. Your birthday? You still haven't said what you'd like, so I'm taking it that you'd prefer to leave it to me, and I'm planning a bit of a surprise, not altogether unconnected with the theatre. Now try and puzzle that one out!

Goodbye, darling. Kiss yourself in the mirror, shut your eyes and it'll be me.

Yours till death do him take,

DICK.

"It begins to frighten me—that last bit," she said as I laid the letter down. "I keep thinking something's happened to him. I even dream he's dead."

"You mustn't give way to that sort of thing," Norris told her. "You've nothing whatever to go on, unless there's more evidence than this."

"Mind if we take a copy of this letter?" I asked her.

I took it through to Bertha to save time. When I came back she was handing Norris the envelope.

"I think there *is* some more evidence. It's on the envelope."

Norris frowned over it.

"Post-mark Dorminster. Time one-twenty p.m." He shook his head and passed the envelope to me.

I had to think quickly. It was as if she were testing us: trying to see what brains we had compared, say, with the police.

"The time stamp needn't agree with the time of posting," I said. "That is, if you're wondering whether he wrote the letter before or after he'd had the telephone message."

I was near, apparently, but not quite there. Something else was being waited for. I hedged.

"Naturally we don't know the time of your out-going mails in Dorminster."

"Of course," she said. "I hadn't allowed for that. But he did write the letter after he'd had the telephone call."

"Why are you certain?"

"The first post goes out at eleven o'clock and the telephone call was just after ten. He was free after ten until eleven, and then he had a form till twelve o'clock, and then he was free for the day."

I said either I was more of a fool than I'd thought or else it was just a bit confusing. Would she mind making it more clear. She smiled.

"Well, if he'd written the letter before ten o'clock he'd have put it in the school box, and that's collected at a quarter to eleven, and it would have been posted at eleven o'clock. So he either wrote it while he was free or else while he was taking a form. He went straight to his rooms soon after twelve o'clock and he would have to go by the main post-office, so everyone thinks he posted the letter then."

"Yes," I said slowly. "But let me go back to my own school-days. If he wrote the letter in the common room, then someone must have seen him. Even if he was the only one free on the staff, people must have been popping in and out. So he wrote it in class. Set his boys to work and then wrote his letter."

"Yes," she said. "That's what was found out. He did write the letter then—at least he was doing some writing while the form was committing some Shakespeare to memory."

"That's extraordinary evidence," I told her. "He had the telephone call and he knew it was taking him to Town on important business—secret business. He must have envisaged having to go away to the Continent, and yet he said nothing about it in the letter."

"As I see it," Norris said, "he didn't expect to be going right away—only up to Town to arrange things."

"What did the police think?" I asked her.

"Well, practically what Mr. Norris said. There must have been two people in it at the least, otherwise there wouldn't have been that letter which came the next morning—the one about going up to Town immediately when he was already there."

"And what was the last you heard from the police?"

"Just that they could do nothing more. Dick had a perfect right to go to Berlin, though not on a false passport. They said that when he did come back to England he'd have to be questioned officially about that."

I thought for a moment.

"Let me put something to you again. Everything you've told us shows that he didn't think he was going to be away for good. The letter shows it. The fact that he didn't even drop a hint. That letter struck you as normal?"

"Perfectly so." The same faint flush came to her cheeks. "We weren't very demonstrative, but that didn't mean we didn't think a lot of each other."

"Practically nothing but theatre in the letter. That was normal?"

"Certainly. He was mad about the theatre and so was I. I'd even thought of getting another job nearer Town, and I might have done if I hadn't been sure we'd be getting married. And I was interested, naturally, in what he was writing."

"Of course you were. But the surprise he mentions in the letter. The one he expects you to puzzle out. Something still connected with the stage."

"I think I did puzzle it out," she said. "I thought he'd be taking me to Town for a day when I came home and we'd do a matinée, perhaps, and then we might even choose an engagement ring."

"That sounds to me like a first-class solution. But looking at everything generally, anything else you've thought of?"

"No," she said. "Unless it was that he'd never have let the school down like that. The Head has never had a single word from him, and Dick was the most considerate person you could ever find."

"All I can suggest is that he'd been sworn to secrecy. I know that sounds melodramatic, but there it is. Nothing else you remember?"

There was nothing. I think I rather surprised her, after catching Norris's eye, by telling her that we'd take her case.

"But we're not going to involve you in any great expense, Miss Crewe. What we—"

"I don't mind the expense," she told me. "I'm what I suppose one calls well off. I don't mind what I spend provided there's an end to this perfect agony of suspense."

I said that we'd work for a week and then present a full report. If we'd no definite news, then it would be for her to decide if we were to persist. That satisfied her: so did the terms. While the contract was being drawn up she gave us various addresses and she signed the retainer cheque. I saw her to the door and managed to get her a taxi.

When I came back I told Norris it looked as if we'd a pretty tough row to hoe.

"What's your own idea about things?"

"Well, frankly, I either think you were right about him going out there to help somebody or else he was a Red. The Commies had something on him and they were going to make use of him. Don't ask me how."

"I hope you're wrong," I said. "I mentioned weekly stages to her because I was hoping he might be back in a fortnight or so."

Norris opened the operatives' book and was ready to get down to business.

"I'll work by myself for the moment," I told him. "Picking the brains of the police is rather a ticklish job. What are your ideas about starting with the Special Branch?"

9

TUNNELLING

I DIDN'T go to the fountain-head and contact the Commander, Special Branch. Since I had no standing except as an ordinary citizen I had to tunnel instead, so I contacted Chief-Inspector

Jewle, with whom I'd often worked before he'd been trans-
ferred. He said he'd do what he could and I arranged to meet
him the next morning at eleven o'clock at a certain tea-shop.

He was on time. As we shook hands there was something
rueful about his grin.

"I don't know, sir, but you'll get me hanged one of these
days."

"A painless death," I told him. "But let's get outside a cup of
coffee. That should cheer you up."

The coffee came, and a plate of cakes. He was wanting to
know just what my interest was in the Alton Case. There was no
point in holding things back, so I told him everything I knew.

"Well, there's no law against a private enquiry," he said. "If
you'll pardon my saying so, though, I can't see you getting very
far. The Dorminster people sucked the orange dry and that's
why they applied to us."

"And what's the S.B. found out?"

"Sweet Fanny Adams. No more than you know yourself. He
left Dorminster and he hasn't come back. He was last heard of
in Berlin, where his letter was posted in the British sector. He
didn't use his own passport. That's about the lot."

"You accepted the idea that he was a Red?"

He grinned.

"I don't think anything's been accepted. We have our own
sources of information and in some mighty high places, but
none of them produced any evidence of his association with
the Commies. Besides, he wasn't a scientist engaged on nuclear
fission and he wasn't at the Foreign Office. As far as we could
make out he hadn't even any contacts with anyone who was.
What earthly good could he be to the Reds?"

"Don't know," I said. "What about the embassies? Anything
from them?"

He looked surprised.

"Come off it, sir. What sort of an answer would we have got?
Whether they had or not, they'd have sworn on a roomful of
samovars they'd never even heard of him."

"Yes," I said. "Sounds as if you've washed your hands of the whole thing."

He shrugged his shoulders.

"My information is that the buck's been passed back to Dorminster. They've probably filed everything and are hoping for the best. That being that he'll turn up again."

"And you people? What's a rough idea of what you think?"

"Well, I gather that as far as we're concerned he's just a young feller-me-lad who had a sudden itch to see what was behind the Iron Curtain. If the Reds want him, then as far as we're concerned they can have him—not that we've any information that he's got any further than Berlin. We haven't any information beyond his letter that he got as far as that. Berlin's a mighty big place. If he does come back, then he'll be asked a few questions. Where he got his passport, for instance. Who his pals were, and so on."

"You really think he will come back?"

He shrugged his shoulders again.

"Don't know. He might turn out to be one of little Bo-Peep's sheep. He's got plenty to come back to. A very nice young lady and more'n enough to live on. I know what I'd choose myself."

That seemed to be everything. I went back to the Agency and talked things over with Norris. Sooner or later I'd have to see the Dorminster police and the present seemed as good a time as any. I thought the Agency should be kept under cover on the off-chance that Dorminster knew nothing of my association with it. Few police look very kindlily on amateurs. When the Broad Street Detective Agency has to be mentioned in his presence, even Wharton looks as if the neighbourhood had suddenly been invaded by a highly unpleasant smell.

We looked up times of trains.

"I'll take the two-twenty," I said. "Give me a start and then ring the Dorminster police and ask for their C.I.D. chief-inspector. If he doesn't know my name, give me a build-up. And give him the impression that I'm a friend of Joan Crewe. Quote yourself merely as an ex-chief-inspector of the Yard and hang up when he gets too inquisitive. Say I'm on my way to see him. As soon as I get to Dorminster I'll give you a ring. You know the time."

Norris didn't look too happy about all the Machiavelli business. I thought of something else.

"Joan Crewe will be back at her school, so try and get hold of her and warn her about my posing as a friend of hers."

"Why not combine the two?" he told me. "She can be a friend of yours, but if you were connected with a detective agency, wouldn't that be all the more reason why she'd apply to you?"

I said he was right. All the same, I'd keep the Agency up my sleeve. The time to produce it would be when I looked likely to be found out. After that I went home and packed a bag for the night, had lunch and caught the two-twenty. It was a slowish train that got me to Dorminster at three thirty-five. I rang Norris from a station kiosk.

"It's all right, sir," he told me. "Chief-Inspector Standing will see you at five o'clock. He knew about you. Nothing apparently about here. I've booked you a room at the White Lion, by the way."

The hotel was five minutes away. It was drizzling, but I didn't take a taxi. At a stationer's I bought a map of the city and a local guide-book. I registered at the hotel and had tea there. Just before five o'clock I was at police headquarters.

Standing didn't look like a policeman. He was tall and his face was fat and florid and his waistcoat bulged. He might have been anything from prosperous tradesman to auctioneer, though his voice was too mild for the latter. He told me as we shook hands that he knew me well by repute. I asked him if that was equivalent to a warning and he laughed. We got on well after that.

"And you're a friend of Miss Crewe," he said. "A nice young lady. Dorminster born and bred. And she thinks you can do something about Mr. Alton?"

"Not quite that," I said. "I promised her to go into things, just to ease her mind. Also it's just possible we might find some new angle. Two heads are said to be better than one."

"That's right, sir—even if they're sheeps' heads. No offence of course." He shook a despondent head. "I only hope we can find something. This affair has set the whole city by the ears. It's got us absolutely beat. It's got everybody beat."

We agreed it might be a good idea if I told him what I knew. He sat there expectantly, an ear cocked for the unexpected and an eye for the rabbit from the hat. He looked disappointed when I told him that was all.

"Just about what we know ourselves," he said.

"Any Communists in the town?"

He gave me a shrewd look.

"Bound to be a few. About ten thousand people voted Socialist at the last election. Two or three of the shop-stewards in the local industries are said to be Red. We couldn't prove any contacts with Mr. Alton, though. He wasn't even a rabid Socialist." He got to his feet. "Look, sir: I have to go out for an hour or so. I'll give you all the statements and you can look over them for yourself."

He produced a file that must have been three inches thick. I made myself comfortable, as he'd told me, and began looking the documents over. When he came back, and that was well over an hour later, I had little that was new and plenty that was confirmatory. The picture of Alton was certainly far more clear.

One or two staider members of the common-room had found him too flippant. One or two had thought his teaching methods too showy, but all agreed that his discipline was good and that no master was more popular. In the common-room his politics had not been aggressive: he had merely cut occasionally into an argument and been strongly for more social and financial equality. That, according to the statement of the senior classics master, was insincere in itself. Alton had a useful private income and had only laughed when asked why he didn't put principles into practice by sharing it out. It was added that he'd been no friend of Russia, though he had occasionally defended some Russian actions and points of view. Politically shallow was how one senior member described him. Everyone agreed that nothing could be more fantastic than that he'd gone behind the Iron Curtain to offer his services to the Reds.

Capon, his closest associate at the school, had been the man of about his own age whom he had asked to do the evening's supervision: he was also a member of the local dramatic society.

"What're you going to do? See a show?" he'd asked Alton.

"Just some business," Alton had said. "It's an idea, though. I could get home by the eleven-thirty."

Everything—Alton's tone of voice, the smile, the anticipation—were perfectly normal. There had been only one other thing. Alton had thanked Capon and gone off with a cheery wave of the hand. Then he'd turned back as if he'd wanted to add something, and had changed his mind again and gone his way. A pencil line had been drawn by that part of Capon's statement and in the margin, probably in Standing's handwriting, was— *What had A. intended to say?* That was something to which there might never be an answer. It struck me as something particularly vital, and it had struck Standing the same way, for he had had a further interview with Capon.

S. This business of turning back, sir. Just go over it again, will you?

C. Well, I thought he was going to say something, so I just sort of waited, and then he shook his head and smiled to himself and went off. That's all there was to it.

S. I don't want to put words into your mouth, sir, but just look back again. You say he smiled. Wouldn't that mean that what he'd intended to say would have been something pleasant? Some surprise or other?

C. Well, it might have been anything. I couldn't possibly say. All I know is that he looked pleased with himself and I thought he was going to speak, and he didn't.

S. In the light of what's happened since you can't suggest anything?

C. Not a thing. As I told you before, Inspector, it's utterly beyond me.

So much for that, and it was folly to tell one's self that if Alton had spoken that morning I should have had no reason to be at Dorminster. But there was one other thing that emerged from the statements made by members of the dramatic society. Alton had actually rung the secretary—a Mrs. Yandle—about an hour before he took the London train.

A. Hallo, Julia: this is Dick. You didn't want me tonight, did you?

Y. No, we're just going over some of the minor parts. If necessary, yours can be read. I told you that.

A. Just thought I'd make sure. I'm going to Town myself. Thought I might finish up with a show.

Y. Lucky you! How's the play coming along?

A. Not too bad. I might let you read it soon after Christmas. . . . Cheerio, Julia. See you on Monday.

She said that about all that there'd been nothing unusual. His tone had been cheerful, but then it always was.

When I'd run an eye over the last of the statements I sat back in the chair, lighted my cold pipe and began to think. As I saw things, I was further off than when I'd started. The whole business was a mass of contradictions.

Alton was young, financially more than secure, happy enough in his work and with never a noticeable care in the world. He loved life and refused to take it too seriously, even among his seniors in a common-room. It was true he had admitted to Capon and others that he'd have liked to be a professional actor, but even that could not have been too serious. With his money he could have afforded to live in Town and haunt agents, managers and authors, and with never a fear of a crust in a garret.

And yet, after a telephone conversation, he had thrown everything up—not for the stage but for a virtual disappearance into thin air. But even up to the last moment he had been as considerate as everyone had described him. He had not walked out on that supervision but had found a substitute. He had taken the trouble to ring Mrs. Yandle and make sure he was not letting her down. And in practically the same breath he had let everyone down—the girl to whom he was virtually engaged, the school, the dramatic society. And why? Had those final solicitudes been a calculated concealment? I didn't think so.

There was only one answer to the why and wherefore of it all: the one I mentioned to Standing when we were again talking things over. Alton had definitely not suspected that he would be away from Dorminster more than the one night.

"That was the conclusion I came to myself," he said. "Say we accept it—then what happened in London to make him change his mind?"

"Don't know yet," I said. "Any chance of seeing his rooms?"

He found the key and we walked the couple of hundred yards to the second-hand bookseller's shop. There was a side door that was open and we went up a flight of uncarpeted stairs to a landing. Standing opened the one door, switched on the light, and we went in.

It was a nice flat: small kitchen with gas-cooker, bathroom-cum-lavatory, one bedroom and a large lounge. The lounge was pretty untidy and just as Alton had left it, but with a fire alight it must have been cosy enough. Sectional bookcases were full and running over. Most of the books were to do with the stage, and there was what looked like a complete set of Mermaid Classics. Even the prints were theatrical ones, and there were three or four old play-bills of Dorminster's long defunct Theatre Royal.

"You have a copy of that letter he wrote to Miss Crewe," I said, "and you'll remember references to a play and a sketch. Are they still here?"

They were. The Queen Anne reproduction bureau was unlocked and he found them both. He told me not to worry about finger-prints. They'd been well examined.

I glanced at the play, which had no title. It was in long-hand and a mass of emendations, but I gathered it was a modern comedy—a weekend house-party sort of thing. I looked at the sketch—*News for Grandma*—and I could have read it in ten minutes. Grandma's news was of a purely imaginary legacy, and the sketch dealt with the way she used it to test out three likely heirs. It was sprinkled with wisecracks, even in character descriptions. They fell rather flat with me, but maybe I'd have chuckled if I'd had a good dinner and been seated in a stall. The interesting thing was that the typed, bound pages I held in my hand were the original.

"Surely he ought to have sent this to an agent and not a copy?" I said.

"Far as we know there isn't a copy," he said. "He did this himself."

I hadn't seen the typewriter, which was in a far corner masked by an easy chair.

"Curious," I said. "According to the letter he has a copy with an agent. Did you check up on that?"

He admitted ruefully that it was the one thing that had escaped him. There were no other papers of consequence, he assured me of that. Electricity had been cut off and as the room was pretty cold we went back to the station. As we walked there I told him that theory of mine about Alton's possible interest in someone he had known in Germany. On that chilly evening it was so fantastic that I wouldn't have outlined it at all had it not been too dark, even under the street lighting, for him to have clearly seen my face. But he seemed extraordinarily interested: maybe the drowning man and the straw.

We didn't go up to his room.

"If you've nothing better to do," I said, "come and have dinner with me at the White Lion. It's almost eight o'clock and we might see things differently after a meal."

So we had dinner together, and over it and coffee in the lounge and a drink or two still later, we threw that case from hand to hand. All along it was that theory of mine that was attracting him. I even began to believe in it myself. I told him it would be a long business if he really wanted to try it out. It would mean interviews with officers of Alton's regiment who'd been in Germany at the same time, and that might be only the beginning. It might mean an enquiry into every German acquaintance.

"Sounds like another job for the Special Branch," he said. "Somehow I don't think they're likely to undertake it."

"If you do approach them, then the theory's your own. Keep my name out of it," I told him. "As for that business of a variety agent, I'll do as we said. It's just possible that Alton may have gone to see him before attending to whatever other business he was in Town for. With any luck I ought to have something for you in a couple of days." When I'd first arrived in the city there'd been at the back of my mind the certainty that I would have to pay a visit to the school. Now Standing had assured me that I'd get nothing new. Statements had been checked and rechecked and the same with the dramatic society.

"I'll take your word for it," I told him. "First thing in the morning I'll get back to Town. I'm rather hopeful we shall pick up a later trail than we have already at that variety agent's. The moment I hear anything I'll let you know."

I got back to Town about eleven the next morning, took my bag to the flat and called on Tom Holberg, a very old friend who has the biggest theatrical agency I know. I didn't have long to wait.

I told him precisely what I wanted—the name of an agency to whom Alton might have sent that sketch of his. Tom pulled a face.

"Doesn't sound like anything an agency would handle. Was it written with anyone in mind?"

I said I didn't think so.

"I can't see an agency handling it," he said. "It should have been written for someone who does that kind of thing. If there were four characters, that makes it even more unlikely. A script writer might have bought it, perhaps, if he had someone in mind."

"You can take it from me," I said, "that it was sent to an agent, and the agent thought he could do something with it."

He still didn't like it.

"Might be some small agency who hoped to sell it to someone. But it couldn't be, unless the author was a fool."

"What d'you mean?"

"Well, the principal character—this Grandma woman—would have to be very good. The good people don't use small agencies."

It ended up with my getting a list of all the agencies from Tom's secretary. That afternoon I put a man on the job and I also went to work myself. It was quick work. The agency area is pretty restricted and there was only a simple question to ask: had or had not a Richard Alton sent them a certain script for sale. By noon the next day we had worked through the list. No-one knew a thing about *News for Grandma*.

I rang Tom Holberg and asked about provincial agencies. He told me to forget it: there was virtually no such thing. So that was that. Even if there had been provincial agencies, Alton, an hour from London, would never have used one. And yet he had used an agency: either that or he was a liar. A white liar, maybe, trying to convince Joan Crewe that that sketch of his had merit. And yet even that was wrong. She had read it herself and she'd assured Norris and myself that it did have merit.

The whole thing was mystery added to mystery. Knowing what I did about that bound script I'd seen in Alton's rooms, I was prepared to swear that it had never been sent to any agency. Surely he would never have typed out two separate copies when one perfectly good carbon would have been practically as perfect. And if he had taken a carbon copy, why send that instead of the original? It didn't make sense. That's what I told Standing when I rang him that afternoon.

The next day's problem was what to do to earn that retaining fee, and for the life of me I couldn't see which way to turn. I spent a long hour with Norris, going over each detail of the affair, and neither of us had any new ideas. All we could think of was that I should go back to Dorminster and hope for inspiration there. But that was before lunch. What I saw in the late morning paper was to make everything very different.

10

ALTON COMES HOME

IT WAS only a paragraph, and I wouldn't have read it at all if the headline hadn't caught my eye.

DEAD MAN FOUND IN DITCH

The body of a fully clothed man was found early this morning in a ditch that adjoins the road from Medlington to Dorminster by Herbert Grapple, an agricultural worker. The body, it is understood, had been for some considerable time where it was found. The Dorminster police began immediate enquiries.

Mind you, I saw no connection with the missing Richard Alton. I had no reason to. Mine was a kind of topographical interest: the fact that this body had been found within the Dorminster boundaries, and the afterthought that Standing would now have his mind off the Alton Case.

I finished my lunch and went back to Broad Street. Norris was out, but Bertha was in the office before I could even take off my coat.

"Dorminster police have been ringing you, sir. They asked if you'd ring them as soon as you came in. The number's Dorminster 2323."

"Get them," I said, "and put me through."

While I waited, Alton was very definitely in my mind: not in connection with that body but with the certainty that Standing had at last unearthed something and was anxious to discuss it. Then the call came through. I was speaking to the station sergeant.

"The Inspector isn't here, sir, but he was wondering if you could get here."

"When?"

"Soon as you can, sir."

"I think I can manage it," I said. "But what's in the wind?"

"You haven't heard, sir? We got the news through to the Press first thing."

"Wait a minute," I said. "Something to do with that body in a ditch?"

"That's it, sir. It's Alton's body."

"But it can't be!"

"That's what the Inspector said, sir. But it is. There's no doubt whatever about it."

I let out a breath.

"Right, Sergeant. I'll be down as quick as I can make it. Probably in the course of the next couple of hours."

"Just a minute, sir."

In under a minute he was telling me that I might catch the two-twenty. Thanks to a handy taxi I just made it, and with time to dash into the flat and throw a few things in a bag. Bertha was booking me a room at the White Lion.

The sun was shining and it was a mild, almost muggy day, so that even the suburbs looked cheerful. To me it might have been any kind of day as I sat in my corner and tried almost frantically to give ideas a wholly new stability. In a minute or two I had a point of reference—the letter which Alton had sent to Joan Crewe from Berlin. If his body had been for some considerable time in that ditch, then he could never have written that letter, a letter that had been posted more than three weeks after his disappearance. And if he had not written it, then someone had written it for him and in order to make it appear that he *was* in Berlin.

I cursed myself for not having asked Standing's sergeant just how long Alton had been dead. It made a difference. Maybe he *had* gone to Berlin and back, and had left the letter with a friend with instructions to post it after a certain lapse of time. If he had come back that much earlier, then why had there been all the secrecy? No telephone message, no. letter, and yet he must have known the enormous anxiety of those on whom he had run out.

The stream of thought was dissipating itself in side channels. I tried to keep nothing in mind but that actual letter. Joan Crewe had said it could have been written only by Alton and because of that reference to *As You Like It*. But wouldn't that knowledge have been shared by a mutual friend? And not even necessarily a member of Dorminster Dramatic Society? And then that thought went, thrust out by something that was suddenly and blindingly enlightening.

Richard Alton had taken it for granted that he would be spending just that evening in Town. I went further: I would have been prepared to bet a pretty big sum that his body had been in that ditch since late that same night or at the most the night after. He had *not* let people down. His actions had *not* been inconsistent. Richard Alton had either been murdered that night in Town or had died under remarkably queer circumstances.

Had he come back to Dorminster by that late train? Surely Standing must have checked up again on that. If he had, then Alton had died in Dorminster and his body had been taken to that ditch. That was the obvious solution. It tied everything in. It left nothing unexplained, except who had killed him and why. A pretty big question, but nothing to the problem that had confronted us before. As I saw it, everything had been localised. Irrelevancies and inconsistencies had disappeared and only one thing remained—a body in a ditch. The intangible had become the tangible and the fantastic had ceased to be there.

After that I could look out at the countryside with thoughts a not too intrusive background. Soon the brakes began to grind. Through the bare trees that lined the embankment I saw the cathedral tower above the massed roofs, then the train swerved to the marshalling yard and in a couple of minutes was slowing to a halt.

Standing was waiting at the barrier.

"Glad you could make it."

The grip of his hand made me wince. We went along to his car and he was hardly seated when I asked my question.

"How long had Alton been dead?"

"Don't know exactly," he said. "We're waiting for a second opinion. Our man thinks best part of a month." He clicked his tongue exasperatedly. "It's the very devil. Throws a proper spanner into the works."

We stopped at the hotel. I checked the reservation and left my bag.

"You'd like to see him?" he asked as he moved the car on.

"Don't know," I said. "What was he like?"

"Pretty horrible. Only the clothes held him together."

I winced again.

"I don't think I need see him. How did you identify him? By the clothes?"

"Yes," he said. "We knew the tailor who made the suit."

He slowed the car and pulled up by the station.

"The Chief's waiting to see you, if you don't mind. We'll go up to his room."

We went up the steps and through the tiled lobby to the stairs. Standing tapped at the door ahead of us on the landing. We went in.

Gilson was a burly man, tough-looking and grizzled: a Chief Constable who'd come up the hard way. There was nothing grim about the smile as he held out his hand.

"Glad to see you, Mr. Travers. I know you by name, of course. Standing tells me you're interested personally in this Alton business."

He offered his cigarette-case. The three of us settled down. I explained what he'd called my personal interest.

"We've sent for Miss Crewe," he said. "She'll be here late tonight. You'd like to know just what's been happening at this end?" He stopped. "What about going out there, Standing? It'll be light for best part of an hour."

I put on my overcoat again and we went down to the car. The Chief drove. We went due south down the main street and over the traffic lights. In half a mile we forked left to a minor road that was little more than a lane. A few bungalows and we were in open, undulating country, arable mostly and interspersed with woodland. Another mile and just short of the first houses of Medlington village, Gilson slowed the car. A uniformed constable was standing by a field-gate and over the low hedge could be seen a couple of men, working methodically along the ditch. We got out. Standing straddled a huge puddle at the open gate, half jumped to the grass and went off for a word with his men.

"This is it," Gilson said. "A field of winter wheat." He waved a hand. "Well up, as you see, but a bit flooded down here. All the rain we've had. And a choked ditch. Just like these damn farmers. Never do a non-paying job till they're forced. That's how the body was found, though. Hewson, that's the farmer, sent a man to start clearing it out. Come round this way and wriggle past the gate-post."

I wriggled round, my long legs straddled another puddle and I was on the narrow grass headland, and I didn't have to move another inch. That soggy grass was trampled in. At the bottom of the deepish ditch—drain-pipes made a kind of culvert for an entrance at the gate—the weeds were flattened to a sort of oasis.

"That's where he was, as you see," Gilson said, "and the devil of a job we had getting him out. What do you make of it?"

It looked obvious enough: his body had been brought along in a car and dumped. That might or might not imply local knowledge.

"This lane much frequented?"

"Just local traffic. Might be used by anyone going home after a cinema or something like that: otherwise not used at that time of night. Goes on through Medlington and Rayfield and then circles round to the main London road. The one that went to the right at the fork."

Standing came back. I asked about checking that late train from Town.

"Alton wasn't on it," he told me. "If he was, then no-one saw him."

I asked if I could state a case. Dorminster—30,000 people— was not like a small town where everyone knew everyone else. Recognition would be largely a matter of social strata.

That train got in at eleven-forty and it went on. Tickets would probably be collected by a porter who was wishing himself in bed. Alton wasn't a regular traveller. Everything, surely, was against recognition.

"You may be right," Gilson said. "It's a possibility. Far as the porter remembers, about twenty people came off that train. None of them recognised Alton from a photograph and description. I admit none of them was acquainted with him."

"How many carriages on the train?"

"Five, and a guard's van. Anything in that?"

I said there wasn't, unless it had been an attempt to visualise the arrival of the actual train. The longer the train, the more straggling the people who went past the porter. Gilson gave a grunt that was almost Whartonian, ran his eye along the ditch and gave it as his opinion that we'd seen everything. We wriggled round the gate-post to the car.

It was dusk when we got back to Gilson's room. A huge tea-tray was brought in. Once more we made ourselves comfortable. Gilson pushed a button on the intercom. The buzzer went and he picked up the receiver.

"Anything down there yet?"

He frowned to himself as he waited. There was the faint sound of a voice. His face lighted.

"That you, Harper?"

The faint voice went on. A minute went by before Gilson spoke.

"If you're dead sure, then that's that. Like to write your report here?"

A moment or two and he was hanging up.

"Harper," he told me. "Senior surgeon at the hospital. He confirms what our own man found. Cyanide poisoning. Taken almost certainly in alcohol."

It shouldn't have been a shock and yet it was. Murder as a hypothesis is one thing and actual murder another. Or hadn't it been murder?

"Nothing against suicide," Gilson admitted. "A motive might turn up. But if it was, then why did someone move his body? You can't say he was drinking with somebody and the cyanide got in by accident and the other one got scared and carted him to that ditch. Things don't happen in that way—not with cyanide."

"Any new ideas on how long he'd been there?"

"Harper won't swear to nearer than between three weeks and a month. Maybe tests on the clothes might tell us something more. We've sent the overcoat to the Yard. The hat wasn't with the body, by the way."

There was a silence as if we were on the verge of something and we didn't yet know what. Then Gilson asked if I'd have another cup of tea. Standing took the tray to the side-table. Gilson passed his cigarette-case again.

"You've got plenty of time, Mr. Travers?"

"All the time in the world," I told him. "I'm here for as long as you think I can be a help."

"That's good of you," he said. "Strikes me we'll need all the help we can get if we're going to make head or tail of this business. So what about starting at the beginning? You agree, Standing?"

The beginning could be taken as the telephone call. Gilson was claiming that it had come from Town and probably from a call-box. That, he said, made it fishy from the start. The call had never been intended to be traced. But it had taken Alton to Town. The news it gave had been far from unpleasant if Capon's evidence was correct, nor had it been ultra-secret. Alton had been smiling when he turned back as if to say something else to Capon. At the last moment he had changed his mind and had not spoken. He preferred, perhaps, that whatever news it was should be a secret for the moment.

Alton, I learned, was a methodical person and reasonably tidy as far as concerned his bedroom. His bed was always made after breakfast, and the bed had been found made when the police had entered. But when had it been made? The morning after his return from Town? We had now to assume that he had never envisaged staying away from Dorminster that night. Every action showed that he was going to Town as a result of that telephone call, hoped to get time in afterwards to do a show, and was then returning by the late train. That he didn't was by no means a certainty.

But he hadn't slept in his rooms that night. The morning post arrived early and he'd have opened that enigmatic letter on which had been built up the theory that he was a Red who had been called to Berlin. There was the same proof that he hadn't returned the following night.

But to get back to the first night. If he had come home, after all, by an earlier train—unlikely though that was—then he might have come to his rooms with whoever it was that murdered him. That implied that the murderer had brought the cyanide with him and had contrived to put it in a drink. But leaving all that for the moment, what of the removal of the body? The street had been well lighted and there was no back way. How then could a body have been brought out to a waiting car without a soul observing it? Cyanide acts in seconds, not minutes. Alton could not have been induced to gulp down a drink, spring down to the car and get in it and then die there.

The street was lighted all night and it had been under the usual police observation. There had been a slight mist, but far from enough to conceal the bringing of a body from the side door, across the wide pavement and into the car, even after midnight when the street was practically deserted. In other words, the conclusion was reached that Alton had been killed elsewhere: at a house, where the car could have been in an unlighted drive or garage entry.

"Right," Gilson said, and wrote something on his pad. "That'll mean enquiring into every friend and acquaintance he had here. Emphasis on the ownership of a car."

"What about his pockets?" I said. "Anything known to have been removed? Tabs cut from the clothes? Any effort made to conceal who he was?"

"Far as we know, none at all. His wallet was there, and everything. Nothing to explain the telephone call, though, or why he went to Town." His eyes screwed up a bit. "Do you think we can discard every idea of him being a Red?"

"The only use I have for the word is red herring," I told him. "I see the whole thing as a kind of subconscious McCarthyism. A reporter comes down here and his paper wants the sensational.

He unearths the fact that occasionally Alton expressed socialistic views. Easy enough to go on: the chap was a Socialist, maybe a fellow-traveller and therefore a disguised Red."

"What about the letters?" asked Standing.

"Red herrings. The murderer knew Alton would be killed that night. The letter couldn't arrive till he *was* killed, and therefore it came the following day. You haven't been able to prove what actual post it came by, so I'd say it was posted in Town the next morning and arrived by the afternoon post. It made an allusion to previous instructions and because it had to explain why Alton hadn't received orders before. Put it this way. I want Alton to be thought a Red. I get him to Town—"

Then I stopped. My fingers went to my glasses—a nervous trick of mine when it seems I'm on the verge of some discovery.

"I think we're all wrong," I said. "I think the murderer wasn't clever at all when he sent that letter."

They both spoke at once.

"How do you mean?"

"Well, I think Alton was lured to Town on some pretext or other and he was killed there. The letter was an afterthought on the murderer's part. He knew about Alton's political or social views and he sent the letter to blind a trail. It was short, cryptic: the perfect touch. He brought Alton's body to where it was found and to give the impression that he had been killed in Dorminster. Later on he followed up the cryptic note with one from Berlin. It wouldn't have been too hard to get someone to post it there."

"Wait a minute," Gilson said. "I don't disagree, but this case had wide publicity. Wouldn't the one who took the letter and posted it have come forward?"

"Possibly," I said. "But couldn't the murderer have been going there himself? After all, there was a pretty long gap between the letters. He might have been waiting till he *had* to go to Berlin. Or, better still, Germany other than Berlin. He could then have given the letter to a German to post in Berlin. A German wouldn't know about the Alton Case."

"Yes," Gilson said. "I'm beginning to think you're right."

"Take both letters," I said. "If further proof's needed that they were fakes, what about the absence of finger-prints? Why should Alton have written that Berlin letter with gloved hands? And both letters were typed."

"Yes, but that letter from Berlin," Standing said. "What about that personal allusion Miss Crewe told us about?"

"The reference to *As You Like It*?" There was no need to think long about that. "Continue logically and you have the answer. The murderer wanted the letter in the same vein as the first: an air of mystery about it. Hush-hush. Sorry I daren't say more at the moment: that kind of thing. But this letter was to be actually from Alton himself, and therefore there had to be a personal allusion. In so much as it used *As You Like It*, it's now a valuable clue. Whoever wrote that letter knew two things: he knew Alton's dramatic interests and he also knew about Joan Crewe. He even knew a combination of both things—that they'd played together in *As You Like It*."

"You're dead right," Gilson said. "Our man's a someone connected with the local dramatic society. That's where we're going to start looking."

"That's it," Standing said. "The real red herring was getting Alton killed in London instead of here. That means the murderer had a house in London. Either that or a business premises. A warehouse or factory or something."

We agreed it hadn't been time wasted. We now had three separate clues. Find a man who had the three essentials and there was the murderer.

It had been a longish session and I got up to go. Gilson said he'd run me to the hotel in his car. I didn't want to do any more talking about the case, so I said I needed the fresh air and I'd walk.

"You said Miss Crewe was coming in late tonight?"

"Yes," he said. "She'll be staying where she generally does when she's here—with a Mrs. Henderson at The Close. A second cousin, or something like that."

I kept the name in my mind as I walked back to the hotel. I looked up the number of the Henderson house and while I had dinner I mentally composed as hard a letter as I'd ever had to write. I had to convey what had to read like genuine sympathy, I had to explain my present position and I had to add a little business. When I'd written the letter I wrote to Norris and asked him to return the balance of the Crewe cheque. I posted both letters in the box at the head office.

As I waited for sleep that night I couldn't help wondering if optimism was justified. After the criss-cross of talk in Gilson's room and the emergence of ideas that had seemed to have behind them both logic and fact, it had been natural to hail those ideas as a kind of final daylight. I, as one of their authors and begetters, had hailed them as such myself. But now I wasn't so sure. Something was telling me that behind that murder had been a brain far too clever to have left what now appeared too obvious clues. If Gilson and Standing had not checked up thoroughly on the local dramatic society already, then they'd been slovenly indeed.

Just as I was falling asleep, a new idea came out of the blue.

It must have merged into other ideas, for, as I said, I fell asleep and I didn't wake till about my usual time. But that idea was in my head, and it wasn't. I had on my mind what I might call the oppression of it: the knowledge that I had thought of something really vital, and yet for the life of me I couldn't think what it was. It was like searching and searching for a forgotten dream.

11

STRANGE ECHO

AFTER breakfast that morning I realised that there was probably little for me to do in Dorminster. Local enquiries were best made by local men, and in the rare event that Gilson might want something from me, then Town was not much more than an hour away. I was intending to ring him to that effect, but it was he who rang me.

"Thought I'd let you know I saw Miss Crewe last night," he said. "She couldn't throw any light on things. She was very upset, of course."

He told me Standing was already at work on the lines we'd decided on the previous evening.

"Just as an afterthought," I said, "there's the question of jealousy, when Miss Crewe's equal to talking about it. Some other man might have been in love with her. And about that Berlin letter. The British forces there have their own newspaper. You might arrange to get an appeal in it for any man to come forward who was given that letter to post."

He seemed to think both were good ideas and the first one the more direct. After all, we had not even thought of a motive for Alton's murder.

"He wasn't killed for the fun of it," he said. "And he wasn't killed for his money because he left everything he had to Miss Crewe. After you'd gone last night I had an idea we might go a bit deeper at the school. Too many brains behind this murder for my liking and those people ought to have brains."

I told him where he could reach me in Town and at what times. There was no great hurry for me to get back, so I had a look at the school, put in an hour at the cathedral and lunched at the hotel before taking a train. After that, life for the next few days was pretty dull. Christmas was coming, but it didn't matter to me if the goose were fat or not. The muggy weather made even the shops into queer anachronisms. Then Bernice came back and things settled into a placid groove.

Gilson rang me once or twice, but always with nothing to report, and I had no new ideas. And so to the week before Christmas. George Wharton and I had been lunching together and it was about two o'clock when we went up to his room at the Yard. It was not for any particular reason: merely a continuation of a walk and behind it the knowledge that neither of us had anything special to do.

The buzzer went before he could even hang up his hat. He laid his pipe on the desk, blew out his lips and picked up the receiver.

"Speaking," he said, and: "Who!"

He scowled away as if he couldn't believe what he was hearing.

"Right," he said, "I'll come down."

"Well, what d'you think of that?" he asked me. "It's that parson, Halsing. They say he seems a bit unstrung."

He went out. Wild ideas began running through my head. Were we back at the Posfort Case? Why else could Halsing have come to the Yard? Had he come with information about the murderer? Had he come to confess? I was so impatient that I went to the door and looked out. I could hear Wharton's voice and I went back to my chair. A moment or two and Wharton was coming in, and he was leading Halsing gently by the arm. Halsing was talking and talking and his voice was a queer monotone. I caught something about the ethics of killing.

". . . clear and defined, my dear sir. You'll find it in the Mosaic law. . . ."

Wharton was getting him to sit down and beckoning to me at the same time. I came across. Halsing had looked clean through me and I might not have been there.

"Get his daughter," Wharton whispered, and nodded sideways towards the door.

". . . an eye for an eye, a tooth for a tooth: that's what . . ."

I caught only that before the door closed. As I went down to telephone I was thinking with a kind of horror of the look there had been on Halsing's face—the vacancy of the eyes, the unshaven jowl and the slight slaver at the corners of the thin lips. At Ralehurst he had looked hopelessly unstrung. Now he looked mad. Either that or he was in the grip of some terrible breakdown. As for the implications, I didn't even try to think. The face and the voice were too vividly near.

I waited impatiently for my number. When it came an unknown voice was on the line. It said that Mrs. Haze was out. Would I like to speak to Mr. Haze? Another minute and he was on the line.

"Travers here," I said, "speaking from Scotland Yard. Your father-in-law's here and he seems to be very disturbed mentally. Can you come along at once?"

"Oh, my God!"

I waited a moment. The news had apparently not surprised him.

"Right," he said. "I'll be there as quick as I can make it."

I went upstairs again. When I opened the door the room was strangely quiet. Wharton was talking gently about some case he had once solved. Halsing's dark felt hat was still on, but he had unbuttoned the overcoat. He was smoking a cigarette and the ash had fallen down the black front beneath the dog collar. He glanced up at me and frowned. Wharton stopped talking.

"My name's Travers," I said. "You remember me, Mr. Halsing? Please don't get up."

He was on his feet.

"Travers," he said, and his head went sideways as he tried to think. "There was a Travers at Oriel. A queer fellow. I believe he became a schoolmaster."

He sat down. The chair wouldn't have been there if I hadn't hastily moved it in.

"You were saying, my dear sir?"

He'd forgotten all about me—if he'd ever really noticed me at all. I caught Wharton's eye and he nodded.

"The diamond robbery," Wharton said, "and how we couldn't get any idea of how the packet had been stolen."

"Yes, yes."

The cigarette had burnt down almost to Halsing's fingers. Wharton moved an ash-tray across while he went on talking.

"It was a real mystery, Mr. Halsing. There was that packet under observation from the moment it was handed in . . ."

I sat quietly watching, an ear cocked for the coming of Courtney Haze. Halsing sat quietly too, nodding now and again as Wharton made a point. He might have been a child, listening to a fairy story. Five minutes went by and Wharton was still spinning his story out.

"So that's how it was done, sir. But I ought to tell you about those two brothers who did the job . . ."

Another couple of minutes and there were voices. A tap at the door and a plain-clothes sergeant was ushering in Courtney

Haze. Halsing got to his feet, face wreathed in smiles. He might have been in his own drawing-room.

"Well, Courtney! What are you doing here?"

"Just going by and I thought I'd drop in. You're having tea with us, you remember."

"Am I?" He looked up for a moment. "Perhaps I am. I seem to forget so many things these days."

Courtney took him by the arm and they went through the door.

"Go with them," Wharton told me quickly. "Find out what it's all about." He changed his mind. "No. Perhaps you'd better let him get to Haze's flat. They'll probably have a doctor there."

"Must have been a pretty grim experience for you, George," I said. "What was he talking about?"

"Damned if I know—nor him either." He gave a grunt. "He had that daughter of his on his mind. Never heard such a lot of gibberish in my life. Still, I soon quietened him down."

"He mentioned Posfort?"

"Never once. And I didn't try to make him. You never know what people in his state are going to do." He glanced up at the clock. "You might get along quietly now and hear what his son-in-law has to say."

I took a police car and drove slowly to Quinton Place. Courtney Haze opened the door almost as soon as I rang.

"How is he?" I said.

"Asleep," he said. "The doctor's given him a sedative. He's coming round again later."

"A nervous breakdown?"

"Yes," he said. "He began to go a bit queer two or three weeks ago. Then last Tuesday was Caroline's birthday and that brought things to a head. My wife went down there and we had a specialist in. He wanted to get him away somewhere for a rest. A nice quiet nursing-home or something like that, but the old boy himself wouldn't hear of it. The next day he was almost himself again." He let out a breath. "And now this has to happen."

"But why should he come to the Yard?"

"Ask me another." He shrugged his shoulders. "Perhaps he had that visit of yours on his mind. The brain's a queer thing when it begins to go a bit rocky."

"Your wife in?"

"It's a matinée," he reminded me. "I expect she'll try and keep him here, though, and have a nurse in. I haven't rung her, of course."

"James still at Ralehurst?"

"Yes," he said. "He's had his leave extended till just into the New Year. He'll be all right, though. There's a cook and a maid to look after him. By the way, what was my father-in-law talking about to you people?"

The question had been just a bit too off-hand, and he had been picking up the cigarette-box. I said I wouldn't smoke.

"I don't think he talked about anything that was really coherent. I caught something about an eye for an eye and a tooth for a tooth and then I went to get into touch with your wife. It's only a guess, but I think he had Posfort on his mind. Superintendent Wharton couldn't make anything of what he was saying."

I said I'd be going, but we'd be grateful if he'd let us know how his father-in-law was getting on. He asked me to apologise to Wharton.

"It must have looked pretty rude of me coming into that room and taking him straight out."

"No-one thought so. It was the very best thing you could have done."

The telephone went.

"Excuse me," Courtney said, and went across the room to the receiver.

"Yes?" he said, and then he suddenly turned his back to me. I was looking out of the window, pretending politely not to hear. Not that I did hear anything except the last words.

"Not at all. You stay put. . . . Yes, everything's well in hand."

"That was James," he said. "He's been out all day and had just got home to find his father gone. Wondered if we'd seen him."

I held out my hand and said I'd be getting along. A minute or two later I was reporting to Wharton from a telephone box at the Underground Station. I could have told him a whole lot of things, now I'd had time to think: reminded him, for instance, of that visit to Ralehurst on a certain afternoon and his doubts about the menacing hostility with which Halsing had received me. As it was I just told him briefly what I'd learned at Haze's flat. I added something else.

"Would you mind if I ran down to Ralehurst straight away? Sort of semi-officially? I'd like to talk to James Halsing now he's alone."

"What's on your mind?"

"Nothing for you to get suspicious about," I told him. "Probably only a hunch. Shall I go or not?"

I went. And I was thinking a whole lot of things as I drove towards Ralehurst. I wondered why Courtney Haze had been so anxious to know what Halsing had been telling us at the Yard. And why he had told James to stay put. I wondered if that nervous breakdown of Halsing's had been caused, not so much by the suicide of his daughter as from the knowledge of Posfort's murderer. Maybe it had been the strain of keeping to himself what he knew of the murderer that had brought on that breakdown. Maybe I had been right in the first place—that Haze himself was the murderer and that his wife's evidence was worth even less in fact than it was in law.

It was just short of four o'clock when I came to the rectory. I drove round the circular drive and backed the car to the porch, heading for home. When I got out I heard a noise like hammering coming from round the far side of the house. I took a look round and there was James Halsing, coat off, the sleeves of the khaki pullover rolled back, hammering something on the concrete drive-in in front of the closed garage. He didn't look disconcerted at the sight of me.

"Hallo, young fellow," I said. "Doing a bit of work?"

"Just straightening out this front mudguard," he said. "Bashed into the back of a lorry this morning. Not my fault, though. The damn driver pulled up without giving a signal."

"I've just come from seeing your father," I said.

"I know," he cut in. "Courtney rang me and said you might be coming down."

This was a facer. And either James Halsing was particularly guileless or else he was equipped with far more brains than I'd given him credit for.

"What about a spot of tea?" he said. "I could do with a spot myself."

He looked at his grimy hands and grinned.

"Looks as if I'd better have a bit of a clean-up too. You won't mind waiting? How was my father, by the way?"

I told him what I knew, and he gave no sign that he'd heard it from Courtney already.

"Hope to God something'll be done about him," he told me. "It's been pretty grim down here lately. Would you mind waiting in here? I shan't be a minute. Give that fire a poke while you're at it."

I was in the drawing-room and it looked and felt different now that I was alone. I gave the fire a stir and put on a knob or two of coal. I looked round the room again and again I liked what I saw. I was even more certain that the portrait above the mantelpiece was a Romney. Then my eye caught the William Kent bookcase. I had not really noticed it before and I went across to examine it. Books were higgledy-piggledy on its shelves: classics in old bindings, paperbacks and books with gaudy jackets.

Then I saw something. It was unjacketed, but on the spine was its title—*The Flying Beacon*. Something like a shiver went through me, and though the house was deadly quiet I held my breath and listened. That bookcase was unlocked, and with one eye on the door and an ear cocked for a sound, I slipped that book into my overcoat pocket. Another minute and the maid was bringing in a tea-tray—a huge pot of tea and three-quarters of a large plum-cake. Before she could set out the cups, James was in the room.

"That's the stuff, Nora. We'll see to everything now."

We settled to tea and talk. That flippant approach of his to life generally didn't conceal an anxiety for his father. Everyone was very worried, he said.

"Looks as if that business of my sister has really broken him up. A pretty hellish business that. Funny, really, I should mention it. The whole thing's been strictly taboo."

"What did he talk about when the bad spells came on him recently?"

"He didn't," he said. "He used to shut himself up in the study or go about muttering to himself. Once or twice he spent a whole day at the church. I don't mind telling you I used to keep well out of his way."

"It may seem a queer question," I said, "but was he much of a reader?"

"Don't know," he said. "He always used to work his way clean through *The Times*. He was pretty high-brow generally. He didn't like novels—modern novels." He smiled. "They tell me he once preached a sermon about them. All sex and that sort of thing."

"What about yourself?"

"Me?" He grinned. "I'm a low-brow. A detective novel or a Western's about my cultural limit."

I refused another slice of cake, but had some more tea. As he carved himself another wedge I was thinking how remote his generation was from my own. There he was, legs well out towards the fire, eating away as if life had never a care: taking my presence there as a matter of course: friendly enough and chatty enough, and I all the time with the feeling that everything was on the surface and that he'd have been just as happy by himself in that world of his so remote from my own. I told myself he'd be a good officer. His men would like him and he'd have the kind of pluck that had no great need of thought.

"You haven't found out who killed that swine Posfort?" he suddenly said.

"Not yet," I told him. "Maybe we never will."

That was when I decided to ask him a question. There had been no need to ask it of those whose alibis were in order. An alibi automatically covers everything. And though his alibi hadn't been accepted as perfect, no question about a gun had appeared on his statement.

"I suppose you never ran across one of those little guns like the one that was used on Posfort?"

"A point two-five, wasn't it?"

"A six point three-five millimetre. Probably Italian."

"That's what we'd call a point two-five in English," he told me. "Not much in my line though. I always carried a Service Webley. Courtney has a little gun. Keeps it as a curio. The one he had in that film of his—*Martha's Husband*." He laughed. "Do you know I saw that film in Singapore? I'd heard about the play, and some of us were in Singapore and we walked into a cinema and damned if there wasn't Courtney! The fellows I was with wouldn't believe me."

I tried to keep the tension from my voice.

"I was just the opposite. I saw the play but not the film. Was it the same scene? He's the ambassador and he's questioning that woman who's supposed to be a British agent. Just as he unmasks her, she dips into her bag for her gun, only it isn't there. He has it and he's pointing it at her."

He laughed.

"That was it. Damn clever, I thought, the way he'd got that gun. The same one he used in the play, by the way. They wanted him to use a property gun, but he wanted the real thing. Then he used it in the film. A sort of mascot."

"When he fired at the ceiling, that was a blank?"

"You mean when he was giving a signal?" He shook his head. "It wasn't a blank in the film. I mean, she'd have meant business. Far as I remember, you actually saw the hole the bullet made."

I sheered the talk away from guns and bullets. For courtesy's sake I finished a cigarette and announced that I'd have to be going. It was dark when we came out to the car. It seemed suddenly to strike him as strange that it should be facing homewards.

"It's a sort of mental tidiness," I said. "Clearing up something before beginning anything else. Besides, I might have been in a hurry to get away."

"A good idea," he said. "I must remember that. It might be useful some time, even with a motor-bike."

There was something of which he reminded me and I thought of it as I came to the straight stretch beyond the village. He was just like a big, lumbering, clumsy but exceedingly friendly Airedale we once had: plucky enough when he thought there was danger, but at other times just a menace to anything that stood the faintest chance of being knocked over.

For the life of me I couldn't see James Halsing behind that Posfort killing. As an accessory—yes; provided the part he had to play hadn't been too involved. Why Courtney Haze had warned him that I might be coming to Ralehurst was another matter. Was there something Haze feared he might let out? If so, it couldn't have been anything to do with a gun. James had talked about that as freely as if we'd been discussing motorbikes. Maybe I'd put that question guardedly to Courtney Haze himself, if Wharton agreed.

I rang him from New Cross, which would give me an immediate choice of ways when I moved on again: back to the Yard or round to Quinton Place. He was in, but he seemed somewhat undecided when I'd told him what had emerged at Ralehurst.

"If I go now," I said, "it'll be a great chance to get him alone. His wife will be at the theatre."

"Come back here," he said. "There isn't all that hurry. I'll get in touch with him and make sure he's going to be in. I can make the excuse to ask about his father-in-law."

It was getting on for seven o'clock when I got to the Yard. As I went in, I was told to wait. In less than no time Wharton was down.

"Think I'd better have a word with this Haze chap myself," he told me. "About time I ran my rule over him."

12

NEW APPROACH

WE WERE in the drawing-room of Haze's flat. Wharton had been expected but not myself, or that's what I had thought when Haze caught sight of me. Before Wharton had come to that matter of the gun there had been polite enquiries about old Halsing. Haze said the doctor had looked in again and Halsing was sleeping soundly. In the morning they were hoping to get him away to a quiet little private nursing-home near Eastbourne.

"You really think all this is due to the shock of his daughter's death?" Wharton said.

Haze looked surprised.

"What else could have caused it?"

"Don't know," Wharton said. He had refused to take off that old blue overcoat of his and he sat hunched in it, although the room was warm. He looked as wide as a wall and about as impenetrable.

"Just casting about for ideas," he went on. "A curious thing, don't you think, that he should refuse absolutely point-blank to give an alibi?"

"If you mean when Mr. Travers came to Ralehurst that afternoon, all I can say is that he wasn't normal even then. This breakdown hasn't been a sudden business, you know."

"So I gather," Wharton said, and leaned forward. "I suppose you don't happen to know where he was on the night of Posfort's murder?"

"I don't. Someone ought to know at the rectory." He hesitated. "Wait a minute, though. Thursday is cook's day off, but Nora, the maid, ought to remember."

"Don't suppose it matters," Wharton said guilefully. "But about this afternoon. I wonder if you'd mind answering a question or two. James Halsing, your brother-in-law, told Mr. Travers that you'd rung him and said Mr. Travers would be coming to see him—or words to that effect. What made you say that?"

Haze smiled: it might have been amusedly or even ironically. The standard lamp behind his chair rather shadowed his face.

"It seemed a natural conclusion. I didn't want James here, as you can imagine, so I told him to stay put. I suppose I was wondering—subconsciously, so to speak—if you people weren't anxious to know why my father-in-law should go to Scotland

Yard of all places. So, as Mr. Travers came here, I thought naturally he might go down there."

"Yes," Wharton said. "Natural enough, as you say. But something else seems to have cropped up—the little matter of a gun. Don't you own a little Italian gun?"

"I do," he said, and to me he seemed genuinely surprised at the question. "I've had it for some time now."

What he told Wharton was almost word for word what I'd heard that afternoon from James Halsing. He added something else.

"I didn't only keep it as a kind of souvenir; I thought it might be useful, what with all these robberies in flats and so on. Normally my wife and I are out till pretty late, and I might just happen sometime to come home and catch some fellow in the act."

"And what was the make of it?"

"Italian."

He had hesitated for the merest moment. Wharton's smile was ironic.

"Now, now, Mr. Haze: what d'you take us for? First you tell us how much you valued the gun and how you'd handled it hundreds of times, and now you don't come out pat with the name."

"I didn't know that it mattered. If you really want to know, it was a Feroni."

"Then tell me this. There was an appeal in the Press for owners of Feronis to come forward. Why didn't you let us know you had a gun of that make?"

Haze shrugged his shoulders.

"Frankly, I didn't see the appeal."

Wharton's sudden gape and the lifting of eyebrows were like an insult.

"You sit there and tell us that you didn't read the papers? You, who'd been up to the ears in the Posfort affair! You saw him at his office. You were acting on behalf of the family, and you want us to believe you weren't even interested enough in his murder to read the papers!"

"Don't put words into my mouth," Haze told him with surprising sharpness. "I merely said I hadn't seen that appeal."

"And if you had?"

"I might have rung someone at Scotland Yard. And I might not. The important thing was that I had nothing to do with Posfort's death and neither had my gun."

"You'd like to show us the gun?"

"Why not? I'll fetch it for you."

He seemed to be gone a pretty long time. Wharton was getting impatient. He got up and stretched his legs. He was still on his feet when Haze came back. And Haze was looking really perturbed.

"Sorry, but I can't find it. The last time I saw it, it was in a drawer in my room, and it's gone. I've looked everywhere."

"Mind if we have a look at where it was?"

We went through a door opposite the small lobby. Haze's room was quite a large den: electric fire, leather chairs, theatrical photographs, knee-hole writing-desk, a rack of pipes and a clutter of papers. It had a faint smell of cigar smoke. A box was on the mantelpiece against a framed photograph of his wife.

"In here," he said, and opened a drawer of the writing-desk. "Some cartridges still there, as you see."

We looked in. Wharton pulled the drawer out. It was a small side-drawer. Behind two boxes of writing-paper was the space where the gun had been. There were five of the small shells. Wharton grunted.

"You say you've looked everywhere else?"

"Everywhere. But why should it have gone from here?"

"Who comes in here?"

"Anybody and everybody," he said. "Men principally, of course. Friends, business acquaintances—everybody."

"And when was the last time you saw the gun?"

He looked away across the room, biting his lip as he thought.

"Yes," he said, as if to himself. "The day after James came home. He lunched with us here and we got to talking about guns and we were in here and I showed him my gun. He wanted to borrow it to have some shooting practice, but I wouldn't let him have it. I know James too well."

"How many bullets were there then?"

Once more there was a hesitation.

"Probably about what there are now. The gun wasn't loaded—I know that."

"Mind if I take a couple?"

"Help yourself."

Wharton put a couple in his wallet.

"Any blanks?"

"Afraid not. We had blanks for the play, of course, but live stuff for the film. I just had the one shot to fire and it had to be real."

"Know where the gun originally came from?"

"Perfectly well," he said. "It belonged to the assistant producer of the play—Michael Deerson. I can give you his address and telephone number if you like."

"Might be as well," Wharton said. "But am I right in saying you asked him for the gun as a souvenir and he gave it to you?"

That was correct. He had given the live rounds as well. It was as he was telling us that that Haze was making a quick correction.

"I seem to think there should have been more rounds than five. I may be wrong, but that's what I think."

Wharton waved a hand and said it didn't matter. We went back towards the drawing-room but did not enter it. Wharton held out a hand. There was the usual spiel about being grateful.

"We'd like to tie up this business of the gun. You could come along to the Yard in the morning some time and make an official statement?"

It was arranged that he should come at about eleven. Another minute and we were on our way out. Wharton didn't say a thing till I had the car moving.

"That chap knows something. Did you notice how it began to dawn on him when we were in that private room of his?"

"Just how do you mean?"

"Mean to say you didn't notice it?" He snorted. "Plain as the nose on your face. He guessed his brother-in-law had taken the gun. He knew Posfort had had six bullets pumped into him, so he began covering up, telling us in so many words that the gun couldn't have been used to kill Posfort because there'd never been six bullets. Then as soon as he told us who'd given him the gun he knew we'd make enquiries about the number of rounds, so he changed his mind. Said some shells might be missing. He didn't say it right out: he said he thought so."

"Did James take the gun?" I asked him. "Was it even taken at all?"

He asked me to go into details, though he must have known what I meant.

"It doesn't need details," I told him. "It's too simple for that. We suddenly appear at Haze's flat and tell him we know he has a little Italian gun. He pretends to find it, but puts it somewhere else. He's probably now dumping it into the Thames. Those few bullets in the drawer were left there to show his good faith."

I concentrated on my driving and left him to think that over. When we got to the Yard he asked if I was coming up to his room. I said there was nothing more I could tell him, but I'd drop in the next morning, just in case.

After a latish service dinner, we had quite a domestic evening at the flat. Bernice had one small table on one side of the fire and was dealing with a big pile of Christmas cards. I had the other small table and was using my fingerprint set to test that copy of *The Flying Beacon* which I'd taken from the bookcase at Ralehurst rectory. I had three sets of prints to work with. At the rectory, I had left a sheet of paper from my notebook on the little table on which I hoped the maid would put the tea-tray, and I had drawn that table suggestively nearer to my chair. She had picked the paper up, asked if it were mine and had given it to me. I had also taken from a newspaper rack a copy of the *Church Times*, which old Halsing ought at least to have handled. James Halsing's prints had been easier still. I had claimed to be ignorant of the comparative sizes of a Service Webley and a 6.35 millimetre and had given him another sheet from the notebook to make a rough drawing.

I found the maid's prints on the *Church Times*, which showed she had handled it when she cleaned the room. A whole series of prints were nobody's but old Halsing's. At any rate I had my three prints for checking with *The Flying Beacon*. In a couple of minutes I was up against a problem. The cover had only one set of prints—the maid's. That meant that she had dusted it and put it back. But that kind of dusting ought not to have removed other prints, and among those prints should have been those of the person who had last handled it. But apparently no-one had handled it. All I could think was that someone had bought it with gloved hands and put it in the bookcase with the same gloved hands, and that, to say the least of it, seemed a highly unusual sequence.

In fact it wasn't right. If that book had been bought, then it would have had its jacket. *The Flying Beacon* was far too recent in publication for second-hand copies to be lying around. And if it were second-hand, then it should have carried traces of the prints of both the original owner and the seller. Besides, the copy I had before me had a look of newness. With gloved fingers I turned the pages and I couldn't find even a dirty mark.

There was only one thing to do: to dust each page and hope for the best. I had tested well over half the book when Bernice announced she was going to bed. I didn't stay much longer. The chances of that other half showing prints were more than slim, and there the facts were. I had in front of me a book which no-one apparently had read or even handled, and that was utterly absurd. There was only one conclusion to draw. Whoever had brought it to Ralehurst rectory had carefully removed every print, or had taken care throughout to handle it with gloves.

Equally important was the absence of the jacket. On that jacket had been a portrait of the author and a brief biography, and Posfort's murderer had needed both. But while that might explain why the jacket had been destroyed, it didn't explain the presence of the book. The whole thing—book and packet—ought to have been burned by the murderer. And yet there it had been, full in the view of anyone who chanced to look. Everything was so inexplicable that when I lay in my bed waiting for sleep I was telling myself that it couldn't be as inexplicable as all that. There just had to be some perfectly simple solution and maybe I hadn't seen the wood because of too many trees.

I woke the next morning with no answers. What I did realise was that that copy of *The Flying Beacon* had now to be my own exclusive affair. George Wharton had been told nothing about the book and that was how it had to stay. I couldn't take it to the Yard and plead forgetfulness: the dusting powder would be only too obvious. And that was a pity. Only a very few people could have had access to that room. Considering the extraordinary absence of prints and the likely reason for their removal, I saw no-one implicated but the Halsings, father and son and daughter, and Courtney Haze, all of whom had been at some time or other suspect in the murder of Posfort.

But there was one other—Roland Haze. He was almost an in-law. He had been at the rectory that very first afternoon I had gone there. And he was in Spain. Or was he?

I looked up the number of Vargo Products Limited, waited till just after nine o'clock and then rang. I asked to speak to Mr. Roland Haze.

"Name please, sir?" a woman's voice said.

"Goodson. Arthur Goodson."

"Hold the line, Mr. Goodson, please."

I waited and waited. I was told they were trying to put me through. The pips went and I was still waiting. I must have been near another set of pips when the voice came again.

"Sorry, Mr. Goodson, but Mr. Haze is away. He'll be back the day after tomorrow. Can I take a message?"

I thanked her and said it wasn't all that important. I was merely an old friend whom he'd probably forgotten. Then I rang off and wondered just what I'd got for my money. The answer was—nothing at all. If it had been Roland Haze who brought that book to Ralehurst rectory, then he could have done it before he left for Spain. How long he stayed there was no matter at all. And so to the same inevitable questions. Why should he or anyone else have brought that book to the rectory? Why need it be tied up with the Posfort murder? Wasn't there somewhere a perfectly simple solution to that total absence of prints?

I gave the whole thing up. It was no concern of mine except as an ordinary citizen. I wasn't on the pay-roll of the Yard. What

I'd done was to lend a helping hand to George Wharton. That was what I told myself. It was what I kept on telling myself, and maybe that was why I had another idea. I spent quite a few minutes trying to wipe some of the dusting material from the book and then I slipped it into my overcoat pocket and went to the garage to collect my car.

I'd expected Wharton to be in, but he wasn't. He was away—that was all they knew at the Yard—so I drove out again and over Westminster Bridge. The morning traffic was in full flood and it wasn't far short of eleven o'clock when I got to Ralehurst rectory. Nora, the maid, opened the door.

"Mr. James in, Nora?"

"I don't think so, sir. I think he's gone off somewhere on his motor-bike."

"Have a look, will you? I'd rather like to see him if he's still anywhere about."

She showed me into the drawing-room. As soon as the door had closed I put that book back on the shelves. Suppose—and it was a mighty big suppose—that book had been planted originally by Posfort's murderer; that it had been a red herring like that telephone call which was intended to lure James Halsing to the Royalty Hotel: suppose all that, then what would be the reactions of the one who had planted it if he or she happened to look at it again and notice the dust that still clung to most of its pages? Would the book be left there or would it be taken away? What that dust was should be known at first sight, especially with Nora's prints standing up clear on the cover. Would it scare the murderer into trying to draw some new red herring across the trail? Certainly if it were removed, then it would be the murderer who removed it. After that, one would have only to check up on those who had had access to the room.

That was what I was hopefully thinking as I stood there by that bookcase when Nora came back.

"I couldn't find Mr. James, sir. Cook says he isn't coming in to lunch."

"Never mind," I said. "I'll see him some other time."

I cast a lingering look back at the bookcase and gave my best smile.

"You much of a reader, Nora?"

She smiled too.

"Not much, sir. I don't get a lot of time."

"That's a good book—*The Flying Beacon*. You ought to read it. Looks as though it's been there some time."

A crude approach, but it was the best I could do. She had a quick look.

"I expect it has, sir. I generally notice any new ones when I dust."

She opened the door for me and we went across the hall. I tried that best smile again.

"Don't you ever get any time off, Nora? Every time I come here you seem to be on duty."

She laughed.

"Oh yes, sir. Cook and I have alternate Sundays and cook has Thursday afternoons and I have Wednesdays."

"A day and a half isn't too bad," I said.

"And I get off an hour or two most afternoons too," she said. "Mr. Halsing's very good about that. On Thursdays, when cook leaves a cold supper, I sometimes stay out till ten."

"Your people live here?"

"Oh yes," she said. "My father's the gardener."

So much for that. I didn't dare pursue it further, vital though it had seemed. Posfort had been murdered on a Thursday night. The cook had been off duty and James Halsing had been in Orpington and then in Town. Had that Thursday night been one when Nora, too, had been out? If it had, then the Rev. Timothy Halsing might have been anywhere. Was that why he had refused to give an alibi? Had he counted shrewdly on the protection of his cloth as a reason for not giving that alibi?

The implications were staggering and the questions endless. He must have been a not infrequent visitor to his daughter's flat at Quinton Place. He could have taken that gun. Knowing the normal Thursday movements of the rectory staff, he could have chosen a Thursday for the killing of Posfort. He could have been back at Ralehurst by the time James, too, had returned. Those were the things I saw, and yet I didn't know. Some things fitted, but others did not. I could imagine that mental derangement coming as an aftermath to his killing of Posfort, but I couldn't somehow see him as the man who'd rung his own son and tried to implicate him in that murder.

But all that, I told myself as I drove towards Town, was Wharton's business and not mine. A little minor prevarication and he could be in possession of the facts. As it happened I got away with it pretty well. He was in his room when I got back to the Yard, and as soon as I went in he was saying, mildly enough, that he'd expected me earlier. Matthews was there, by the way.

"I called in at about ten, but you were out," I told him. "And before I forget it, there's something you ought to know about. We were rather rushed last night."

His eyes popped a bit when I told him what I'd learned from the maid.

"The son won't be there at the moment," he said, and gave Matthews a look. "He went with his father to that nursing home only a few minutes ago. You might get down there, Matthews, and get the truth about that Thursday night. The quicker the better. Have someone with you and take statements."

Matthews went out. I was glad it was he and not Wharton who'd probably be discovering that I'd only just returned from Ralehurst myself.

"How was old Halsing, George?"

"Clearer in his mind, so I gathered. Quite amenable to going into that nursing home. His heart's a bit groggy now, so they tell me."

"And what about the gun?"

"Ah, the gun," he said, and leaned back in his swivel seat. "Looks as though we're beginning to get somewhere."

13
THE DISCOVERY

"HERE's the report from Ballistics," Wharton said, and rapped it with his knuckles by way of emphasis. "What I'm open to bet is that Haze's gun was the one used on Posfort. It all adds up."

"What about the bullets?"

"Wait a minute," he said. "Let's get things in their right order. Deerson, the one Haze says gave him the gun, backs up everything Haze says." He shrugged his shoulders. "Whether Haze got hold of him and did a bit of prompting is anybody's guess. I don't think so, though: it's all too simple. Deerson, for instance, says he gave Haze the gun to use in the film because it had already been used in the play. Deerson brought it home from Italy as a war souvenir, but he had no ammunition with it.

"Go back to the play. Haze had to use blanks, so Deerson got him some—"

"Just a minute," I said. "It was as easy as that? You can buy Italian ammunition in England?"

"Yes, just as easy as that. Forget that word *Italian*. What you want to buy is 6.35 millimetre ammunition. So you just walk into any good gun-smith's and you ask for it. It's called 6.35 millimetre auto-pistol ammunition. The equivalent here in inches is point two-five. The bullet weight is fifty grains. There's no tax on it and a box of a hundred costs you thirty-four shillings."

"Right, so Deerson bought blanks for use in the play. But the film was different. Mind you, they needn't have used live stuff. They could have faked it, as you know. Just fired a blank and then done a camera shot showing a hole in the ceiling. But that didn't suit Haze. He was temperamental. What Deerson calls a stickler for realism. Said he couldn't do that scene properly unless he was firing real stuff. You've got that?"

I said it was a masterpiece of lucidity.

"Don't know about that," he said, "but it's what happened. The man in charge at the film studio didn't know how much live stuff would have to be fired before the director was satisfied with the scene, but he actually bought twenty-five. As far as can be ascertained, about seven or eight were used. When everything was over, Haze took the gun and what was left of the live stuff. Deerson had given him the gun, you remember, as a souvenir of the play. And that brings us to this.

"In Haze's drawer there should have been a gun and either eighteen or seventeen live rounds. There were only five there when we saw that drawer. What I think is that there should have been seventeen, and the one who took the gun helped himself to a dozen rounds as well."

"Logical enough," I said, "and I see what you're getting at. Maybe I'm thick in the head, but there's something I don't see. Six bullets were pumped into Posfort and they were all that Ballistics had to go on. Then how were they able to plump for the gun being a Feroni?"

Wharton shrugged his shoulders.

"That's their job. It's child's play to them. I do know they used various automatics of the same calibre and tested the bullets against those used on Posfort. After that they plumped for a Feroni."

"They should know," I said. "So we act on the assumption that Haze's gun was used on Posfort. But surely Haze didn't use it himself?"

"Oh? And why not?"

"Well, the number of bullets isn't right. Let's say that Haze put seventeen in that drawer with the gun after he'd finished the film. There were five when we were there. Six were used on Posfort. What happened to the other six? Surely they weren't what you might call trial rounds, let off by Haze to test what sound they might make in a room. Haze must have known every-thing there was to know about that gun. He wouldn't need any trials. But whoever took the gun might have wanted six spare bullets for a try-out."

Wharton wasn't having it. His favourite for the Posfort kill-ing was obviously Courtney Haze.

"But let's admit I'm wrong," he said. "If he didn't do the job himself, then he knows who did. If not, why did he change his mind about the number of bullets in that drawer?"

He laid down his pipe and got up.

"Look," he said, "I'm Haze. I know perfectly well the police are looking for a Feroni. I've discovered my own Feroni's missing and some bullets, and that as good as tells me who took the gun and how he used it. My policy now is to keep my mouth shut and hope the police never know I had a Feroni. If they do happen to discover I had one, then I'll have to cover up. I'll leave the five bullets there in any case, just to show the gun used to be there.

"All right. I tell the police the gun has gone. Just the gun. No bullets. That lets out the one I'm covering for, or so I'm damn-silly enough to think. No bullets, no shooting. But then what happens? I get a question fired at me about where I got the gun from. I see no point in not answering it. Then I see what I've been fool enough to do. The police'll make enquiries from Deerson and he'll say I had about a dozen and a half bullets. What can I do? Pretend I'd forgotten just how many there were? And hope for the best?"

He sat down again. Histrionically it hadn't been a bad performance. He'd used a drawer of his own desk by way of illustration and over his face had gone the expressions which he was visualising on the face of Haze.

"Right, George," I said. "I'm ready to be convinced. Haze is covering up for someone. For whom? If Posfort's killing was revenge for Caroline Halsing, then the list is extraordinarily short. Roland Haze has an unbreakable alibi, so he's out. That leaves old Halsing and his son James. I don't know what you think, but as suspects I hate the sight of both of them. James knows plenty about guns, but I still don't think he'd have hung about the hotel after he'd killed Posfort. As for his father, the whole idea's somehow abhorrent."

"There we are, then," he told me with a droop of the lip. "We're back at Haze himself. He's the one for my money." He scowled. "Damn all actors anyway. You can't get at 'em. Professional liars, that's what they are when you get down to it. You can't tell when they're acting and when they're not."

"You'll never pin anything on Courtney Haze," I told him. "First of all, there's who he is—right at the top of his profession. His alibi's worthless in law because it's established only by his wife, but look who that wife is. No jury'd ever doubt both their words. The D.P.P. would never let it get as far. Something else has got to be found, and don't ask me where."

"I'll find it," he said, but there was no real conviction in his voice.

It was about time I was going. As I put on my overcoat I tried to do a bit of consoling.

"Were just in a bad streak, George. Everyone gets it sooner or later. Held up on the Posfort Case, nothing from that Rickson Case, and"—on the spur of the moment I decided to unloosen—"as far as I'm personally concerned, that Alton Case. That murder at Dorminster."

"What d'you mean?" he was almost hurling at me. "What's the Alton Case got to do with you?"

I told him perfectly frankly. His eyes wrinkled a bit at the mention of the Agency, but he couldn't do anything about it. The Yard had been called in on that case, he said, and he gave me the names of the chief-inspector and the detective-sergeant who were down there.

"Funny," he said, and shot me a look. "I don't remember your name being mentioned."

I said it wasn't funny at all. The police down there wouldn't be too happy about any reliance on an amateur. And with that I went out. I did tell him from the door that if he or anyone thought I could be a help, then they knew where to find me.

I had thought of going to the office, but I changed my mind and drove home instead. From the flat I rang Ralehurst rectory. A woman's voice answered—probably the cook's. I asked if an Inspector Matthews was there and if so, might I speak with him.

"Tell him it's Scotland Yard."

"Oh dear, what next!" I heard her say as she laid the receiver down. I heard her receding steps and in less than no time the approaching steps of Matthews.

"Travers here, Matthews. I expect you've unearthed that I was down there this morning doing a bit of private work."

"Yes," he said. "I was keeping it under my hat, though."

"Go on keeping it there," I told him. "What the Old Gent doesn't suspect he won't worry about. Any news?"

"Yes," he said, and his voice lowered. "Our young friend *was* out that evening. After she'd cleared away the tea she was given the evening off."

I thanked him and rang off. I had some tea myself and got my pipe going. Bernice was out, and I stretched my long legs towards the fire, sat back in my chair and tried to fit in Timothy Halsing as the man who'd killed Posfort. In a few moments I was weighing the evidence. He had no alibi for that evening. As far as I knew, he had no car, so he would have had to come to Town and return by train, and that could be checked. It was he who might have put that *Flying Beacon* in the bookcase after removing the jacket.

But what he couldn't have done, or so it seemed to me, was conceal his identity. He could never have been the man at the Royalty desk. That patrician, Forbes-Robertson face with the lofty forehead and the deep-set eyes could never have been moulded into anything resembling the Corland of the jacket of *The Flying Beacon*. And as I worked that out, the telephone went. It was Wharton, telling me about Timothy Halsing's alibi.

"Matthews is staying down there and making a few more enquiries," he said. "I'll let you know in the morning if anything else turns up."

My guess was that Matthews would be making enquiries at the railway station, but I didn't say so. I just thanked George and hung up.

My old nurse, a brisk, shrewd but kindly soul, who lived till well over eighty, was always hurling aphorisms at my young head. If, for instance, I was finicky over my food, it would be:

"There's many in the churchyard who'd like to be eating that." If I grumbled at some youthful misfortune I'd be told that nothing was so bad that it couldn't be worse. In what to me were a series of disasters I'd be consoled with the information that it never rained but it poured. I was thinking of that last the following morning, and what I'd told Wharton by way of consolation. In the past he and I had not often had an utter failure. Now we looked like counting the Posfort Case among the misses. And, on top of that, the Rickson murder—a failure because it had been a kind of hit-and-run affair; something into which it had been impossible to get one's teeth. Then, for me, as I'd told him, there'd been the Alton Case. Three misses on end. It hadn't been just raining: it had been pouring.

I was in the office that morning. We had had a call from one of the big stores to supply extra help to their own detectives during the last days of Christmas shopping, and Norris had gone along to fix things up. I had got tired of thinking about unsolved murders and trying to reach up a hand into the nothingness of air and bring down a something out of the nothing, so I tackled *The Times* crossword to keep my mind off things. I was getting along fine when the buzzer went.

"Miss Crewe is here, sir," Bertha said. "Can you see her?" Just for a moment the name had meant nothing.

"Miss Joan Crewe? . . . Send her in, Bertha, will you?" Bertha ushered her in. I could read no tragedy in her face: there was only the same quiet manner and the poise.

"How nice to see you," I said. "Do sit down."

"I'm not stopping," she said. "I only came to thank you personally for what you did."

"That's extremely nice of you. But do sit down. I'm sure you're not in all that hurry. . . . A cigarette?"

"Well, thank you. I think I will."

I held the lighter across the desk and she leaned towards it. Her eye must have caught that crossword and pencil at the side of the desk where I'd hastily pushed them. She smiled.

"You're a crossword fan, Mr. Travers?"

"Yes," I said. "I admit it. And that you've caught me wasting the time of the firm."

"I love crosswords. I'm always doing them. I used to like acrostics, too, but you don't see them often nowadays."

"I remember them," I said. "They used to appear in the fashionable weeklies. But tell me, what're you doing in Town?"

"Some shopping, but really I'm looking for a flat."

"You're thinking of living in Town?"

"Yes," she said. "I've given up that teaching post and I'm thinking of trying to get into one of the dramatic academies. I'm a bit too old, but I hope someone will take me."

I had to smile. *Old*, I said, was a very relative term.

"One of these days I'll be seeing your name in lights," I said. "If you want a thing badly enough, you're bound to succeed."

"I do want it badly." Her face was suddenly older. "It's what I've always really wanted. Now, after what's happened, I'm going to do it."

I found nothing to say. The smile came, very gently, to her face again.

"A week ago I couldn't have talked about what happened, but I can now. I'm afraid I've been just a bit deceitful. I did come to thank you for that very nice letter of yours and for what you've done, but I also wondered if there was anything, perhaps—well, anything you could tell me."

I said that unhappily there was not. I hadn't a single new idea. The local police had called in the Yard, but if anything new had been discovered I should probably have heard of it.

"I'm not vindictive—you must believe that, Mr. Travers—but it was a fiendish thing to do. It wasn't as if Dick were some awful person, for he wasn't. He was fine. And he was young."

"Whoever killed him will be caught. You can rest assured of that. Sooner or later something will turn up. It always does. About that play of his, by the way. Are you doing anything with it?"

"Not at the moment. I might perhaps try to do something later." She laughed quietly. "I'm not so bad about ideas, but I can't quite get them down on paper. But that reminds me of something. You remember *News for Grandma*? I know it was all mentioned in the report Mr. Norris sent me, but have you discovered anything since?"

"In what way?"

"Well, the name of the agent to whom it was sent."

"Afraid not," I said. "We made what we considered the most exhaustive enquiries. Every known agent was questioned, some by me personally."

She shook her head bewilderedly.

"I just can't understand it. He said definitely that he'd sent it to an agent and he'd had a reply. Why should he say that if it wasn't true? There was no need to say it. You couldn't even call it a white lie."

I smiled wryly.

"I know. We took all that into account ourselves. We were just as disappointed as yourself. Agencies can't live on failures."

I thought of something.

"Mind if we have a look at that letter again? It's just possible we missed something; some shade of meaning, perhaps, that might throw a different light on things."

Bertha brought in the Crewe file. I took out our copy of the letter.

"I'll bring your chair round here," I said, "and we'll go through it together. First we'll read the letter right through. You're sure it's not going to distress you?"

"No," she said. "I've been reading it over and over again myself."

Darling Joan,

How are things with you? About the same, I guess, as they are here. Work gets a bit boring and I occasionally wonder if G.S. thinks me as good as he once did. Not that I'm very anxious. Rain goes on monotonously most days and that gives one ideas that are apt to be depressing— not that I'm that kind usually. Did you sniff, darling?

Rehearsals are quite good fun and make an exciting break. Don't forget your promise to get here by hook or crook for the first night. Haven't had time to do a lot to my play, but I like what I have done. We'll have a crack at it together. Something's wrong, as I told you, with that first act. It's too mechanical. How and why, I don't know, but that's where you might help.

By the way, I had a letter about *News for Grandma* from a variety agent recently. Generally one doesn't expect quick answers from people like that, but there we are, and he seemed to think something could be done with it, which is promising, to say the least of it.

But enough about that, darling. Your birthday? You still haven't said what you'd like, so I'm taking it that you'd prefer to leave it to me, and I'm planning a bit of a surprise, not altogether unconnected with the theatre. Now try and puzzle that one out!

Goodbye, darling. Kiss yourself in the mirror, shut your eyes and it'll be me.

Yours till death do him take,

DICK.

"Well, there it is," I said. "Any comments?"

"Yes," she told me promptly. "I always get back to that surprise and how he told me to puzzle it out."

"He expected you to puzzle it out?"

"He must have. And I've thought and thought and I can't find a clue. I'd thought what I told you, about having lunch in Town and doing a show . . . and perhaps buying an engagement ring. But it couldn't be that. You can't have a puzzle unless you have a clue. Besides, at half-term and holidays we often went to Town and did a show. That wouldn't be a surprise."

"What about the engagement ring? Had he ever given a hint about that?"

"No," she said slowly. "Not really. Besides, that wouldn't have been a birthday present."

I was thinking what a cool, logical brain she had. And then something struck me.

"Dick—Mr. Alton—knew about your being fond of crossword puzzles?"

"But of course! He was always laughing at me about it. You see, he hadn't that sort of mind."

"Did he laugh when you won any prizes? Or didn't you?"

"Occasionally," she said. "Years ago I won two prizes for acrostics, and about three months ago I was lucky with the *Spectator* crossword."

"And 'Ximenes' in the *Observer*?"

"I've never been lucky. I've sent several in, but I just didn't happen to come out of the hat." She smiled. "Not that one really wants a prize. It's always quite a lot of fun."

"True enough," I said. "Let you and me look at this in the same spirit. Is there anything hidden in this letter that you ought to have puzzled out? Any anagrams, for instance? Have a good look yourself."

She pored over it, taking it word by word. I did the same, standing behind her chair. We must have spent ten fruitless minutes, taking tails of words, connecting them with the beginnings of following words and trying to find some vital new word from the parts. Then she happened to look at her wrist-watch.

"Heavens, I must fly! I'm supposed to be meeting a friend at half-past eleven, and it's almost that now."

There was no taxi, so I walked with her to the nearest bus stop.

"I don't think there can be anything in that letter," she had told me as we walked along. "If you haven't the brain for solving crosswords you can't very well make them up. Don't you agree?"

I did agree.

A moment or two and she was asking if I would let her know if anything should turn up about that variety agent. I said I certainly would. She reminded me that she'd be staying for the next two days at Black's Hotel.

A bus came in sight almost as soon as we'd turned the corner. She gave me a smile and a wave and ran. I waited where I was till the bus passed me, and she waved again and smiled as she went by.

*

Back in the office I took the Crewe file from the drawer where I'd put it and I was just about to take it back to Bertha when I thought I'd have another look at that letter. Bertha brought in coffee and I lighted my pipe.

I went through that letter word by word, trying to find the unusual. If it was there, it escaped me. Then I tried to assess that letter as a whole. Joan Crewe had said that neither Alton nor herself was demonstrative, and certainly that letter, except for the word *darling*—and even that was promiscuous enough in stage circles—was hardly that of a young man who was very much in love. To me it was a self-centred letter. It was interested in the affairs of Richard Alton, and almost exclusively so. As far as I could judge, it had never a bit of anxious or protective love about it: no wish to know what she was doing and no protestations except that rather flippant ending. Maybe, I told myself, I was old-fashioned. Alton, James Halsing, Martin Collier—all with a kind of protective colouring; all with their own approaches, acceptances, taboos and fetishes and jargons, so different from mine.

My pipe had gone out. I lighted it again and took a last look at the letter. It was that definite statement about a variety agent that began puzzling me again. *And then I saw something.*

In a minute I had seen it twice, and after that there was a long minute when I saw nothing and my mind was a blank. I was holding my breath, or so it seemed, and then I got to my feet. I sat down again, and then I was able to think. Five minutes later I was calling through to Bertha.

14

VARGO PRODUCTS LIMITED

WHAT had happened was this. Though I had glanced for the last time at only a part of that letter, the whole of it had been in my subconscious mind. The part at which I had glanced had been that statement about the sending of *News for Grandma* to a variety agent and the receiving of a reply. It was that beginning of a sentence—*Generally one doesn't expect*—that had suddenly struck me as unnecessarily stilted. It conflicted with the general conversational tone of the letter as a whole. Then, almost before I knew it, my eye had caught what preceded it—*Variety Agent Recently. Generally One* . . . The subconscious mind or eye had made a connection of those initial letters.

In a flash I was testing that letter from the very beginning. At once there was something else: another stilted something that should have been noticed, about the rain going monotonously on. As far as I remembered, it hadn't gone monotonously on. There'd been only a day or two of really heavy rain—the rain that had flooded that wheatfield—and before it the weather had been comparatively fine. But there it was—*Very Anxious. Rain Goes On* . . .

That was all there was, and more than enough. That letter was the puzzle that Joan Crewe had been invited to solve. Richard Alton mightn't have had a crossword brain, but he had brains enough to compose a letter that could be taken as genuine except for certain hints. The puzzle itself and its mnemonic form was something any schoolboy could have contrived. Stripped of non-essentials, that letter consisted of two words—Vargo. Vargo. That's what had taken me so aback. Vargo. Vargo Products Limited. Roland Haze. The Posfort Case. Could that be the sequence? Could the two murders be tied up?

That was what had flashed through my mind before I had really been able to think. After that there wasn't any doubt. That was why I had sent Bertha out to buy copies of all the cheaper illustrateds. When she came back it was with half a dozen. Three of them carried the latest Vargo advertisements. This time I didn't skip the letterpress: I read the whole thing.

The one I had seen previously had carried two photographs, ostensibly of Churchill. The latest carried what were apparently two photographs of a well-known comedienne with a big part in a weekly broadcasting feature. Readers were asked to spot which of the photographs was the real thing. A tab attached to any pound jar of BREKFAST marmalade or BREKFAST jam had to be sent with the letter, and the first three correct competitors drawn from the hat would receive prizes of five pounds, two pounds and one pound respectively. A consolation voucher for a free jar of marmalade or jam would go to the next forty-seven.

What I had thought that November morning, when I had somewhat carelessly looked at the photographs of Churchill, was that that advertisement had been a lone one. Now I was gathering that it was a fortnightly feature. The winner of the previous competition—he had apparently been the very image of Sir Gordon Richards—was announced as a Mr. H. Ossley, of Rooks Way, Oldminster, and he had received a cheque for ten pounds. I wondered how long that competition had been going on, and my finger went to the buzzer for Bertha to get Vargo Products Limited. Then I changed my mind. That could come later. What was important was to think the whole thing out.

A minute and I was going back to Queen's School, Dorminster. In some idle or impish moment Richard Alton had sent in his photograph for one of those competitions. (I made a note. Find out at Dorminster if a special photograph was taken, and when.) Probably he had virtually forgotten all about it, and then on a certain Thursday morning he was called to the telephone. (Find out if it was the custom for Vargo Products Limited to ring their successful competitors.) If he was rung merely to be told he had won ten pounds, why did he consider it necessary to go to Town that afternoon?

As I asked myself that, I knew I was getting far too involved. The one vital thing was that photograph. Whom did Richard Alton think he resembled? And resembled so closely that he stood a chance of winning ten pounds in a Vargo competition. At once I was buzzing through to Bertha and asking her to get me Black's Hotel.

I asked for Miss Crewe and was told to wait. Two or three minutes and I was being told that she was out. What to do then I didn't know. What I did know was that I had to do something. So I put that copy of Alton's letter in my pocket and one of the illustrateds that had carried the Vargo advertisement and told Bertha I was going out to lunch. It was about half-past twelve when I got to Piccadilly Circus, and I walked from there to Black's Hotel. I looked through the lounges and there was no sign of Joan Crewe. I asked at the desk and they rang her room. After that I settled down in the lounge that looked into the main entrance and prepared to wait.

It was a quarter-past one when she came in. She looked surprised, and then almost frightened at the sight of me.

"You've had lunch?" I said.

"Yes," she said. "With a friend. She had to get away early."

"Mind if we go up to your room?"

She led the way towards the far stairs. She stopped suddenly. "Why are you here? Is it something you've found out?"

"Yes," I said. "Something we ought to talk over."

We went into the room. It was larger than I'd expected, and there were a couple of chairs which I drew in at the small table by the side window. She laid her bag and the two small parcels on the bed, and I could feel her trembling as I touched her arm.

I went over that letter with her and showed her what I'd found. Vargo conveyed nothing to her at all, so I showed her the advertisement. I pointed out the definite connection with the letter. Somehow she still didn't quite get the point.

"But even if he *had* won ten pounds, that wouldn't have been a surprise that had anything to do with my birthday. After all, it wasn't as if he needed ten pounds to buy a present with."

"Admitted," I said. "But let's get down to very simple facts. Take the photograph he sent in. It has to be a very close resemblance to some famous person. All we have to know is, what famous person."

She frowned.

"You can't think of any well-known person whom he resembled?"

"I can't," she said. "Not in real life, I mean."

"Then what *do* you mean?"

"Well"—she gave a little deprecatory smile—"we did think there was something when we were doing *Much Ado About Nothing*. It was on in Town at the same time and we went to see it. I saw it two or three times. He was Benedick and so was

Courtney Haze, and he modelled himself on him exactly. It was really uncanny. Every mannerism and almost the same voice."

"He really looked like him?"

"Absolutely like him. He really began it as a kind of rag, and then he decided to take it seriously."

"Quite amusing," I said. "He played Courtney Haze playing Benedick. How tall was Dick, by the way?"

"Five feet nine," she said. "It's a good height for the theatre; not too short and not too tall."

Then she was turning in her chair and staring.

"You don't mean that Dick sent in a photograph of himself as Courtney Haze!"

I couldn't let things go further. I began putting that letter and advertisement back in my pocket.

"I want to ask you to do certain things," I told her quietly. "The most important is, to trust me."

"But I do trust you."

"That's nice to hear," I said. "The next follows. I don't know what's going to come out of all this, but I do know that it's all got to be extraordinarily secret. You'll have to promise me here and now that you'll never divulge a word of what we've just been discussing until I let you know to the contrary."

"Let me ask a question," she said. "Has all this anything to do with what happened to Dick?"

"In my judgment it has everything to do with it."

"Then I promise. Provided you do let me know some time what happened."

I had to impress on her again that most urgent need for secrecy. Scotland Yard would be handling things from then on and it was not unlikely that later they would want a confidential interview.

"Just one thing you can do as soon as you get back to Dorminster," I said. "Have you a photograph of Dick as Benedick?"

"No," she said, and hesitated. "I think I'd like to tell you why. It was because I thought Dick was too attentive to the girl who played Beatrice that I quarrelled with him."

"Don't reproach yourself," I told her gently. "But the photograph. Is there anywhere I can get one?"

She told me the secretary of the dramatic society might have one. That was what I gathered, for she didn't finish the words. Her lip was quivering and the sobs were racking her as I went quietly from the room.

My club was only five minutes away and I telephoned from there to the yard. Wharton was in. I'd said I'd be taking a taxi and I'd be with him as soon as I could. Not that I'd expected many. He knew my unblushing curiosity and he'd probably been wondering why I hadn't turned up long before to ask what had happened at that morning's interview with Courtney Haze.

That's what I did ask him as soon as I was in his room.

"He just made the statement," he said. "Nothing different from what we heard yesterday, except that he thought a dozen or so bullets were missing with the gun." He picked up his pipe and regarded it ruefully. "Funny sort of chap. You find yourself liking him one minute, and the next minute you're sure he's leading you up some damned alley."

"Maybe he is," I said.

He looked up.

"What d'you mean?"

I drew up my chair in alongside his at the desk and laid down that letter and advertisement.

"Something I've stumbled on, George. You remember I told you about a Miss Joan Crewe who was my client in the Alton Case? Well, she came to see me this morning."

It must have taken me a good quarter of an hour to go over everything with him. There were things he had wanted to say, but I made him keep them till I'd finished.

"Remarkably suggestive," he said, and pursed out his lips. "But wouldn't a competition like that be a bit too lowbrow for a chap like Alton?"

"If you mean vulgar—possibly yes," I said. "But his wasn't an ordinary entry. And what you've said explains something— the time lag. Alton wasn't likely to read the cheaper illustrateds and see those advertisements when they began, and that's why he didn't send in an entry till a long time later, after he'd just happened to catch sight of one. After all, as I've just told you, I hadn't seen them myself till a few weeks ago. But the point I want to make is that his wasn't an ordinary entry. He was mad about the stage and he was sending in a photograph of an actor. I don't think he had the ten-pound prize in mind. I think he hoped the sending of that photograph might put him somehow into touch with Haze and so lead to something important to do with the theatre. Even some kind of professional job."

"How would it put him in touch with Haze?"

"That's what you'll have to find out at the head office of Vargo. But surely Vargo Products couldn't publish a photograph of a living celebrity without getting the permission of that celebrity, especially as side by side with it would be the photograph of quite another person."

He gave a grunt.

"As you say, we can find out. And if they did have a photograph from Alton and did get into touch with Haze?"

"Some of that we know already," I said. "In my judgment that telephone message that took Alton to Town could have come only from Vargo Products. Therefore they'd had the photograph and were proposing to use it."

"Very well," he said. "But exactly what could they have told him that made him go to Town?" He gave a little snort. "Don't tell me he was so excited about the likelihood of getting ten pounds that he rushed off to Town to spend it in advance?"

"Look, George," I said patiently. "Let's get down to brass tacks. What you're thinking and I'm thinking is this: whatever was said over the telephone, it was Courtney Haze whom Alton went to Town to see."

"Why?"

"Because Haze's name must have been mentioned and Alton knew he'd have to follow up his luck by a personal interview. That gave him an excuse."

"And then?"

I was getting exasperated. I was a winkle with George manipulating the pin.

"You tell me for a change," I said, and got out my pipe.

He picked up his own, stoked it and took his time over lighting it.

"That's simple," he said, "even if it's melodrama. If he did see Haze and Haze saw the likeness, then Haze used him to establish that alibi at the theatre. That's why Haze—or Alton really—didn't come in till the curtain was rising and that's why he went out just before the end of the act. He didn't want to be seen when the lights were full on."

"That's it," I said. "And after that Alton had to be killed. He went back to Haze's flat. Nobody would be there but Haze himself, and Haze mixed him a drink. And that was that."

"And what about removing the body? Did Haze have a car?"

"That'll be for you to enquire into," I said. "Maybe he had some arrangement with a car-hire or drive-yourself service. But that's how it must have happened, George."

"Don't like that word *must*," he said. "You may be certain, but I'm not . . . as yet."

"Very well," I said. "You're not certain. You think it a coincidence that Posfort and Alton were both killed on the same night."

He started like a shying horse. That was something that had slipped his memory. He bluffed his way out of it. He hadn't been as close to the Alton Case as I had.

"It makes a difference," he told me. "It begins to tie in. But wait a minute. There was something on my mind. . . . Oh, yes. That word Vargo caught your eye because Haze's brother worked there. Or was connected with the firm. Where does the brother come in?"

"He doesn't—necessarily. I take it, though, that people there would know well enough that Courtney Haze was his brother. When that photograph came in they may have shown it to him and he mentioned it to Courtney. That's merely a suggestion. You can get all the answers down there. Roland Haze, I happen to know, isn't due back from Spain till tomorrow."

"Yes," he said, and he licked his lips as if they were smothered in cream. "Looks as if we might have a nice little surprise for our actor friend. No use getting him here till we're practically sure."

He rang down and asked if Matthews was in. They located him in the Special Branch, where, curiously enough, he'd been doing a job in connection with that Berlin letter in the Alton Case. Wharton told him to wash that out. We were on to what might be a short cut.

When Matthews came in it took another ten minutes to explain what the short cut was. Matthews would begin enquiries into the matter of Courtney Haze and a car.

"Don't trust a soul but yourself," Wharton told him. "If even a sniff of this gets out, then he'll have covered up."

Matthews went out. Wharton looked up at his watch.

"Getting on for four o'clock. We'd better get a move on if we're going to that Vargo place."

"You want me with you?"

He looked surprised. I was about to ask him if I was going officially when the buzzer went.

"What the devil now?"

He picked up the receiver. A moment and his tone had changed to the unctuous.

"How are you, sir? . . . *I am* sorry to hear that. . . . You're sure? . . . Well, I can only say I'm sorry. These things have to happen, you know. . . . Yes. Goodbye."

He put the receiver gently down. He looked at me, the clamped lips extending to a sneer of a smile.

"Talk of the devil. That was Courtney Haze. Letting me know he mightn't be available for a bit. His father-in-law's had a stroke. Cerebral haemorrhage. He says he's no chance. Haze's wife has just gone down to the nursing home and he may be going later. Depends on what happens."

He rang down for a car. I put on my overcoat and held his for him.

"Maybe it's the best thing that could have happened to old Halsing," I said. "I can't help wishing I'd known him before all this trouble took place. I wonder what he was really like then?"

"Why worry about him?" George said. "He never was a suspect, was he? Better get a move on or the damn place'll be closed before we get there."

There was a driver, and I sat in the back with Wharton. I'd missed lunch and I looked like missing tea, and I lighted my pipe to stay the gnawings of an empty stomach. We discussed methods of approach and hit on the right ones. Outside the car were the slowly passing suburbs: lighted shops and people on pavements and halts at pedestrian crossings or traffic lights, and everything seen through the faint mist of a muggy dusk. It was a good half-hour after we had left the Yard that the car suddenly turned right. Another minute later it was coming to a halt.

Wharton got out, hunched his shoulders against the chill of the mist and stood looking round. I joined him. A four-storeyed building rose sheer above the tarmac, its windows lighted. Away to the left stretched a long line of lower buildings, the light of their windows more distant and diffuse. Scarcely heard against the noise of the traffic on the road we had just left was a whirr of machinery. In front of us was a flight of six wide stone steps, well lighted from above. At the top were two pairs of wide, glazed doors.

"A pretty big place," Wharton told me quietly, and still he didn't move. Maybe he was feeling, as I did, that we might have come to the end of a road, and he had to get the feel of things in his very bones and take no new step till he was sure.

Then he gave a grunt.

"Might as well go in. I'll do the talking."

As I followed him up the steps I was thinking there'd been no need to remind me of that. A door swung in as he pushed it and we went through. I blinked in that sudden glaring light of the lofty, tiled entrance hall, but ahead of us I saw stairs on the right and what looked like lifts on the left. From somewhere was coming the tapping of typewriters. A couple of men came down the stairs, one carrying papers in his hand. He gave us a look.

"Anything I can do for you?"

"Yes," Wharton said. "Where's your advertising department?"

"Second floor and turn left. The lift's just there."

Wharton said nothing as we rode up. We turned left and there was a door marked ENQUIRIES. A few seconds later a young typist was taking us three doors along. Wharton, by the way, had refused to give a name.

She tapped at the door and looked in.

"The two gentlemen, Mr. Tweed."

Wharton went in. I told myself that this was it. Unless every deduction had been wrong, within a few minutes we ought to know the name of Posfort's murderer.

15

THE PRICKED BALLOON

It was a beautiful office—for where and what it was: rubber-floored in a pale-blue-and-white check, white-tiled for its first five feet of wall and pale-blue for the rest. The very large white desk was flat-topped and the swivel chair was an ivory white. Outside the door should have been a warning notice—YOU ARE NOW ABOUT TO ENTER A ROOM THAT PERSONI-FIES VARGO PRODUCTS. Spotlessness, cleanliness, absolute purity—that was that office. You could have heated its white radiator to bursting point and to work in it would still have given me the shivers.

Tweed wasn't in white. He was wearing a dark suit that looked a bit worn, and, come to that, he looked a bit worn himself: a man of over fifty, whose bald, domed skull was buttressed by two patches of greying hair above the prominent ears. His grey-ing moustache was untidy, and there was a crumb at the corner of his mouth as if he'd just sent out a tea-tray. He took off his rimless glasses and blinked a bit as Wharton went towards him with outstretched hand.

"Mr. Tweed, we're from Scotland Yard. We've come here to ask for your help."

Tweed's eyes bulged a bit. He even hesitated a moment before he took Wharton's hand. He put on his glasses again to read the warrant card. The smile was tentative.

"I don't know what you want, Superintendent, but will you sit down. This is all most unusual."

There was a trace of cockney in his speech. I didn't realise it till much later, but there was some queer difference between him and that room. But I was drawing up a chair. Wharton gave his a look as if wondering if it would bear his weight.

"This is a confidential matter, Mr. Tweed, and we'd like you to keep it so. We're looking for a certain man, and our information is that we might get his whereabouts through one of those advertising photographs of yours. You're in charge of advertising here?"

"Yes, sir." Tweed said it with a touch of pride. "I'm in complete charge."

"Good. Then we've come to the right spot. And you know what advertisements I referred to."

"Yes. Certainly. At the moment we're only running the one."

"And how long has it been running?"

"Just about eighteen months."

"That means you've published some forty photographs. But tell me about it. How did the whole thing start?"

"Well"—Tweed smiled modestly—"I thought of it myself. We'd been doing the usual thing—various things, in fact—and then this idea came to me. I've been working on it one way and another ever since."

"It's bringing results?"

Tweed's smile was expansive. He waved a hand.

"There's the sales chart for the last twelve months, gentlemen. I think it speaks for itself."

Various photographs in white frames were hung round the two shorter sides of the room. Tweed's desk was between the two tall windows of a longer side and facing him, behind us, was an immense graph that showed a gradual upward curve. A subsidiary curve beneath it in red was probably the expense account.

"That's fine," Wharton said. "But how does the whole thing work? Just tell us what happens during, say, any particular week."

Tweed enjoyed those next few minutes. He sat back in his chair, finger-tips together, and every now and again he would give himself a little congratulatory nod. It was all very simple, he said—at least now the whole thing had become organised and virtually automatic. Two kinds of letters were received—those containing photographs and those guessing which of two previous photographs was the real thing. The proportions of those letters were now one to a thousand. He dealt personally with all letters containing photographs and his staff with the rest.

"One to a thousand!" Wharton said. "That's a big difference, isn't it?"

Not at all, Tweed told him. As many as twenty thousand guess letters might be received, but rarely as many as twenty with photographs.

"Wait a minute," Wharton said. "There's a catch in this somewhere. I can get a prize for guessing which photograph is the real thing. What's to stop me sending in two guesses? Then I'm bound to be right."

Tweed chuckled.

"I know. That's just the point. Every entry has to be accompanied with the proof of the purchase of a pound jar of marmalade or jam. All we have to do is ensure that the same person, or anyone from the same address, doesn't get two prizes. It's getting photographs that's becoming the difficulty. Don't forget, gentlemen, that we've already exhausted about forty celebrities. That's why a week or two ago I came to the decision to throw the competition open to celebrities no longer living. Already we've had Gladstone, Kitchener, Roberts, Irving, Marie Lloyd, Lloyd George, Rudolph Valentino—well, no end. It's opened a wide field, as you see."

"It would do," Wharton said. "But what are the fancies among people still alive?"

He chuckled again.

"Charlie Chaplin used to inundate us at first and we had to do one to get rid of him. And to bring in a rule that no make-up was allowed. The photograph of an entrant has to be as the person normally is. But the wireless, that's what everyone goes for. All the big names in wireless and television. Photographs in the *Radio Times*—that's what makes their faces known. And tell me this, gentlemen. Take people who've never appeared on the wireless or television: judges, lawyers, painters, a lot of authors and even some actors and actresses. Are their faces familiar to the man in the street? Not a bit of it. Nine-tenths of those submitted to us have had their photographs in the *Radio Times*—and pretty often. Cricketers and footballers as well, of course."

"That's understandable," Wharton said. "But let's say you get a photograph that you decide is really like that of some living celebrity. What do you do?"

That was slightly more complicated. Politicians were reckoned fair game. Cartoonists didn't have to ask their permission, nor did anything so innocuous as that fortnightly competiton of Vargo Products Limited. Other celebrities were always courteously approached and, if amenable, produced the particular photograph of themselves which they preferred to have reproduced. After that the competitor was photographed by Vargo's own specialist photographer in the same pose and with similar lighting conditions until the twin photographs were virtually the same.

Wharton turned to me. Was everything clear? I said it was perfectly clear. Mr. Tweed's explanations had been most lucid. Tweed simpered behind the pressed finger-tips.

"Right," Wharton said. "You keep every photograph that's sent in, Mr. Tweed? Whether you use them or not?"

"Every single one, sir. They're all filed."

"Splendid! Now this is what we want you to do."

He took a paper from his pocket.

"We're after a certain man, as I told you. This may sound sheer nonsense to you, but the man we want had what they call a stage complex. Keep it under your hat, but we want him not only for fraud but for what's likely to be a very serious charge. But about that stage complex. He always took a stage alias and made himself out to be a well-known—or reasonably well-known— actor. Where you people come in is because he boasted that he'd had his photograph as the real thing in one of your competitions. We got that from one of our sources of information. And we don't happen to have anything like an up-to-date photograph of the wanted man ourselves. What we want to know is if you have any photographs whatever in your files of any of the actors—there're four of them—whose names are on this list."

The spiel had been deliberately long and improbabilities clouded with words. Tweed showed only an enormous curiosity as he took the list. He put on his reading glasses and he frowned at it.

"Would you mind if I passed the question on?"

"Anything you think best," Wharton told him.

Tweed pressed a button on the intercom and picked up the receiver.

"Miss Cherry? Oh, Miss Cherry, I want you to go most carefully through the photograph files and see if we ever had any photographs of the following."

He read the four names. He repeated them and told her to ring him back. He replaced the receiver, opened a drawer and brought out a cigarette-box.

"Sorry I didn't ask you two gentlemen if you'd smoke."

He chatted on while we lighted the cigarettes. His tone was much more intimate.

"One of those names I did remember—Sir Ralph Richardson. We had two of him, but neither was good enough. But about Mr. Courtney Haze's name. It's funny about that. One of our directors is his brother."

"Really?"

"Yes, sir. Mr. Roland Haze. His family have been connected with the firm since the beginning. He's been in Spain the last few weeks. We have big interests there, as you gentlemen can imagine. He'll be surprised when I tell him about this man you're after. He's due back early tomorrow."

"What!" Wharton half-rose from the chair, chin well out and his voice a rasp. "Get this straight, Mr. Tweed. You'll tell no-one! Wasn't the first thing I told you when I came in this room that everything was confidential?"

"I'm sorry, sir. I'm really sorry. I'm afraid I forgot. The peculiar circumstances—"

"Damn the circumstances," Wharton told him. "You let out a single word of what we've talked about this afternoon and—"

The buzzer went. Tweed grabbed the receiver.

"Yes? . . . Only two of Ralph Richardson? . . . You're sure? . . . Hold on a minute."

He cupped the receiver.

"Tell her to check again," Wharton told him curtly.

"Check again, Miss Cherry. . . . Don't argue. Check again."

The voice at the other end was still rumbling as he hung up. He spread his palms.

"There can't be any mistake, gentlemen. Every photograph we've ever received is there. It's child's play to check up."

"Anyone else have access to the files? Could photographs be removed?"

"Why should they be?" He leaned towards Wharton, hands vibrating. "I've got what they call a photographic memory. I've been on this job since the start of it, and every photograph's been through my hands. That's why I spotted Ralph Richardson's name, and the number of photographs. And why I knew we wouldn't have the others."

Wharton said nothing. He stubbed out the cigarette in the desk ash-tray and then the buzzer went again. A couple of minutes later we were getting to our feet. Tweed came quickly from behind the desk.

"Well, we're grateful to you," Wharton told him. "You've done all you can. That Richardson check may be a help. I don't know yet. The two men who sent it don't look likely, though. Remember that other thing I told you?"

Tweed didn't need reminding. Not a word was going to pass his lips and he would caution his Miss Cherry to keep quiet too.

"The very way to make talk," Wharton told him. "Let her think what she likes. You're the boss of this department, aren't you? We may have to come here again. Heaven help anyone who's been doing any talking. We keep an ear very close to the ground, Mr. Tweed."

Tweed said nervously that he guessed as much. Wharton permitted himself to relax. He held out a hand.

We set off back to the Yard. Wharton hunched in his collar and feeling, I knew, like a bear with a sore head. We must have been travelling three or four minutes before he opened his mouth.

"Well, that cooks that goose."

"Something's wrong," I told him placatingly. "There just has to be. You agree that Alton sent in a photograph for that competition?"

"Then where is it?"

"I don't give a damn where it is. I know a photograph was sent. That letter proves it. Also I'd be prepared to bet anything that Courtney Haze knew it. It was he who rang Alton that morning and got him to come to Town. Everything says so. Take the matter of secrecy. Haze told him not to tell a soul. That's why Alton wrote that cryptic letter *after* Haze had rung him. That's why he turned back that morning to give a hint to Capon, that friend of his, and then changed his mind. Haze had to tell Alton not to mention a word. Haze knew how he was going to use Alton and what would happen to him."

"Prove it. Show me that photograph."

"Actions speak louder than photographs," I told him. "I never knew a case that ties up so. Alton goes to Haze's flat. Haze pumps him about himself. Hears about Joan Crewe, for one thing. Hence the Berlin letter later on, and because he'd gathered that Alton was a bit of a socialist. Maybe Haze made himself out to be very left-wing and Alton ingratiatingly followed suit. It was an experience for Alton. He'd have been induced to talk and talk. Haze could have turned him inside out before he broached the scheme to him about trying him out on a real impersonation."

"The body," Wharton said. "If Matthews gets anything about using a car that night, then we can see."

I'd said my piece and I sat back in my corner. I began thinking of possible loop-holes in Tweed's organisation, but I couldn't get away from that photographic memory of his and how he had personally handled every photograph that had ever come in. And then I thought about Tweed himself. Something, somewhere, wasn't right. I couldn't put a finger on it, but there the feeling was, like a vague depression on the mind. Then I almost pinned it down to the suspicion that Tweed wasn't the man for his job, or that office. He looked and spoke like a senior clerk, not a man who was holding down a job worth surely at least fifteen hundred a year.

Or was I wrong? I decided I was. Tweed *was* holding down that job. If that sales graph was any index, then he was right on top of that job. And yet that queer feeling persisted. Something about Tweed himself hadn't been just right. And that was all the thinking I did, for the car was turning into the Yard.

We went straight up to Wharton's room. His clerk heard us and followed us in.

"A message for you, sir, from a Mr. Haze. It's on your desk."

Wharton went straight to it. He handed it to me. It said simply that the Rev. Timothy Halsing had died that afternoon at five o'clock.

I spent my evening at home. There had been no point in staying on at the Yard and spending useless time in still more talk. I didn't want any private thinking. There comes a kind of saturation point when things go wrong, and you find yourself on a mental roundabout, so I busied myself with this and that. Just as I was thinking of bed, Wharton rang. I knew he'd been having a conference with what he calls the Big Bugs.

"Can you drop round in the afternoon?" he was asking me. "About half-past two? I'm seeing a certain person at his flat at three."

"I'll be there," I said. "Anything from Matthews?"

"I'll tell you about that when I see you," he said. "Nothing of what we wanted, though."

I was dead on time. Matthews was there and he gave me his usual grin. I wondered if he'd found something after all. He had, and he hadn't. Haze and his wife, it turned out, were excellent clients of a hire-service firm in Carter Street, about two hundred yards from their flat. When they were playing, a car, or cars, would take them together or independently—it depended on the nearness of the particular theatres—to the West End and call for them after the shows.

"And why not?" Wharton said. "It all went on the expense account. The wife had a car that night. Haze didn't. That doesn't say he didn't get one elsewhere."

"But what about getting the body in?" I said. "How was it brought from the flat to the car? Someone must have been about. Think of it; Haze lugging someone as big as himself down the stairs or to the lift and out to a car. It just couldn't have been done."

"He might have been killed *in* a car," Matthews said. "There's such a thing as offering a chap a drink from a flask. If Haze was driving, it'd have been a good excuse for him not having a drink at the same time."

"It may be a wild idea," Wharton told me, "but we're imagining that Haze offered to drive Alton back to Dorminster and that Alton was killed on the way."

"But you've still got to find the car."

"I know we have," he said testily. "And it won't be easy. That's why we're paying a call on Haze this afternoon. I'm putting certain things up to him to get him a bit rattled, and then there'll be someone on his tail to see if there're any special reactions. Also he might talk a bit too much and let something out."

Bridget Halsing, he said, had been with her father when he died. Haze had gone to the nursing home immediately after hearing the news and had brought his wife back with him.

"He was down there this morning, he and the son, getting the body to Ralehurst and making funeral arrangements and so on. That's why he isn't available till this afternoon."

Matthews left to carry on his search for a certain car. Wharton fidgeted for a bit and then said we might as well be getting along. I hadn't been sure that he wanted me, but I wasn't sorry that he did.

He rang down for a car. Even before we moved off he was telling the driver to take it steady.

"What's going to be your approach?" I asked him.

"The Alton Case," he said. "Might change my mind when I see him, though."

It was only a ten-minute drive at that time of the afternoon and with luck at the traffic lights. We had five minutes to spare when the car drew in at the long parking-place to the left of the main entrance. Wharton got out, looked at his watch and then up at the sky. There was no sun, but there was never a trace of mist, and but for a brisk wind that whirled the dead leaves along the tarmac it might have been an afternoon of late autumn. There was the sound of a plane in the sky. It came into sight and we watched it for a moment.

"That reminds me," I said. "Haze's brother is due back from Spain this afternoon. Or it might have been this morning."

Wharton grunted something and moved off towards the entrance.

"Know what their flat costs the Hazes?" he asked me as we walked up the wide, carpeted stairs. "Eight hundred a year. I took the trouble to find out."

"You chose the wrong profession, George."

He gave me a look which I wasn't seeing. George has always fancied himself as an actor, and it's one of his blind spots to think that nobody knows it.

16

REVELATIONS

WHARTON had to ring twice before Haze admitted us. He was wearing a dark grey suit and his face was looking a bit sallow and his eyes too dark. He didn't offer a hand as he showed us in. His tone was almost curt.

"I don't know what it is that you want from me, gentlemen, but perhaps we'd better go to my room. My wife's just getting up and we don't want to bar the other room from her."

He opened the door to that den of his and we went in.

"A very distressing business for both of you," Wharton told him. "A bit sudden too."

Haze waved a hand at the chairs.

"Sudden, yes," he said. "Probably the best thing under the circumstances. He never recovered consciousness after the stroke. You'll smoke? Cigarette? Cigar?"

"If you don't mind I'll have my pipe."

Haze pushed the two boxes to one side, for my pipe was out too.

"I've got a mouth like a sewer," he told us. "Far too much smoking. This has been the very devil of a time for me. Couldn't have come at a worse time, in fact. Up to the ears in rehearsals—" He broke off. "Still, you don't want to listen to my troubles. I take it you've some of your own or you wouldn't be here."

"I wouldn't say that," Wharton told him mildly. "We just happen to have run up against something unusual. Remarkably unusual. We'd like to hear your comments on it."

"Really?" The eyebrows lifted slightly. The smile was definitely ironic.

"It's to do with that missing schoolmaster, the one whose body was found in a ditch near Dorminster. I expect you read about it."

"A missing schoolmaster." The irony went. The smile was a puzzled one. "I remember something, but not much."

"You remember his name?"

"Frankly, I don't."

"Alton. Richard Alton. Remember it now?"

"In a vague sort of way—yes. But what about him? I mean, what's it to do with me?"

"You're a man of even temper?"

Haze looked at me. I gave a slight shrug of the shoulders. Maybe Haze thought Wharton was getting a bit senile.

"I suppose I'm the average. Why?"

"Because I'm going to put a very personal suggestion to you," Wharton said, "and I want you to take it in the right way. Now take this Alton. He'd done some amateur acting at Cambridge and he did a lot more at Dorminster. He was mad about the theatre. He did some writing for it. He had a private income and he wanted one little chance in order to throw everything up and become a professional actor. That's not very unusual. The queer thing is this. He had a very marked facial and bodily resemblance to yourself."

"Really?" The eyebrows lifted again, but the smile was still puzzled.

"Yes," Wharton said. "You must take my word for it. But to review events. On the morning of November the 10th he received a telephone call at the school and at once he was getting the afternoon off to go to Town. He went to Town and he was never seen alive again."

"Yes?"

"Now comes a somewhat wild hypothesis. November the 10th, Mr. Haze. The date recall anything to you?"

"November the 10th." He frowned, then he stared. "That was the night Posfort was murdered."

"Exactly. So let's suppose. Suppose it was you who intended to murder Posfort and you had everything planned. Suppose it was you who got this Alton to Town and used that facial resemblance of his to give you an alibi at the theatre that night. How's that for a suggestion?"

Haze's lip had curled. Then he laughed.

"Let me make a suggestion. You an opium smoker?"

"Not yet," Wharton said amiably. "But what I'm telling isn't exactly a dream. He *was* rung up. He *did* resemble you. He *did* come to Town that evening and he was never seen alive again. And that evening Posfort *was* murdered."

"Listen," Haze said, and leaned forward. "I'm a damn-fool to take this seriously, but let me assure you of something. Let *me* give some facts. Before I read about his murder I'd never heard of him in my life. And I've never been in Dorminster since—well, about five years ago."

"That, of course, you're prepared to swear."

"If I'm forced to—yes. I should still consider it an insult. But perhaps you'll tell me this. How am I supposed to have known this Alton?"

"Very simply. Through the firm of which your brother is a director—Vargo Products Limited."

"Are you mad or am I?"

"Neither, I hope. But let me explain."

He went over the whole thing, and in detail.

"You see the possibility, Mr. Haze? Let's imagine what might have taken place. Your brother or the man Tweed rings you or tells you that a photograph has come in that closely resembles you and what are the firm to do about it. Would you like to have it published in the usual way? You say no. But you get this man Alton's name and address because you've seen a way you can use him. I don't say for a moment that it's true. All I'm showing you is that it's not outside the bounds of possibility."

The lip curled again.

"Truth stranger than fiction—or is it the other way about? No use, I suppose, my assuring you that my brother never mentioned such a photograph? Nor anyone else. Frankly, I very much doubt if there was one."

"Nobody else at the firm mentioned a photograph to you?"

"Good God, no!"

His cheeks had an angry flush. Something else was on the tip of his tongue, but it stayed there. It was as if he'd suddenly had some startling idea. He frowned to himself. Then all at once his head went slightly sideways as if he was listening.

"I think that's my wife." He was getting to his feet. "Will you excuse me for just a minute?"

He went quietly out. Wharton tapped his pipe on the ash-tray and gazed at it reflectively. My pipe was cold long since and I put it in my pocket, and there the two of us sat, saying never a word. For all we knew, Haze might be listening.

Three minutes went by. Wharton had his eye on the mantel-piece clock. Five minutes had gone when he too began to listen. The flat was very quiet and the sounds that came distantly through the window made it somehow more quiet still. Another minute and Wharton began to hoist himself from the depths of the easy chair.

"What's happening? D'you think he's bolted?"

"He's the world's biggest fool if he has," I said.

And then there was definitely a sound and we sat quickly down again. The door opened. It was not Haze who came in but his wife. We hastily got up again. She was wearing a dark costume and against it her face looked remarkably pale. She gave me a quick smile of recognition, but it was to Wharton that she spoke.

"Superintendent Wharton?"

"Yes, madam. And permit me to say straight away how sorry I was to hear of your loss."

"That's kind of you," she told him quietly. "It was very sudden. We'd hoped he was going to recover. But I came really with a message from my husband. I don't understand it myself, but no doubt you will. He says will you go back to Scotland Yard and he'll be there as soon as he can. He hopes it won't be many minutes."

"He had to go out?"

"Yes," she said. "He didn't tell me what for. He looked very upset about something."

Wharton let out a breath.

"Well, we'll get back then."

Even he was feeling a bit uncomfortable as we followed her to the door. I moved just ahead of her and opened it.

"Mr. Travers," she said. "You haven't been worrying Courtney again about that business that you came here for some time ago?"

"Just wanting some information," I told her. "We thought he might be able to help us. Apparently he can."

She looked relieved. She was smiling faintly as we said goodbye.

Wharton moved quickly along the carpeted corridor and down the stairs. He slowed as we went across the big entrance hall and lengthened his stride again once we were outside. The driver barely had time to open the car door.

"Did you see a man come out about five minutes ago?" Wharton was asking. "Five foot nine or so: had a dark grey suit on. A man of about forty."

The driver hadn't spotted him.

"Wait here a minute," Wharton told me, and back he went to the front entrance. It was five minutes before he reappeared, and then he came round by the car-park on the other side.

"Just as I thought," he told me. "A couple of other exits."

He got scowlingly into the car. Before we were out to the road he was firing the expected question.

"Has he bolted or hasn't he?"

"Why not wait and see?" I said placatingly. "Another few minutes can't make all that difference. In any case you can pick him up more or less when you want him."

He told the driver to move a bit faster. Then he was rumbling away again.

"The damn cheek of the fellow! We're to wait for him! Who the devil does he think he is?"

I left the question in the air. To tell the truth, I wasn't perturbed at all. What I was feeling was almost an excitement. In the course of the next half-hour something would have to happen. If Haze had really bolted, then we were at the end of the case. If he hadn't, then he'd be coming to the Yard and telling us the reason for his queer conduct. It was in that last that I was interested.

But we were drawing in at the Yard. Wharton told me to go up to his room and he'd be there in what he called a couple of jiffs. It was about ten minutes before he actually appeared.

"Thought I'd take precautions," he told me. "I've got three men at the exits to those flats with a description of the wife. If Haze has skipped, she might be meeting him somewhere."

He sat restlessly down, looked at his watch and checked it with the clock.

"How long do you make it since his wife said he'd gone?"

"Just over half an hour."

He began getting up. The buzzer went. He sat down again.

"Yes? . . . Oh! Well, send him up."

"He's here," he told me. His lip curled. "Now we shall hear something."

Haze was ushered in. Wharton said nothing. He looked at him as a father might look at a young son who'd returned nonchalantly home long after the usual time for a meal. Haze couldn't help but feel the hostility. He gave me a look.

"Sit down, Mr. Haze," Wharton told him with an ominous quiet. "Very good of you to look us up."

"May I take your overcoat?"

"Thank you," he said, and gave me a quiet smile. "I know all this must have seemed unpardonably rude, but I don't think you'll judge me too badly when I tell you my reasons."

It was at Wharton he was looking as he sat down. Wharton just sat there waiting.

"Under the circumstances I couldn't say a word to my wife and I didn't dare run the risk of telling you what I could have told you in case she might overhear. And I was far from sure that I ought to tell you. It was almost like hiding behind some-one else's skirts. That's why I went out. I thought I'd take a quiet walk by myself and think things over."

"And all that boils down to what?" Wharton said curtly.

"That I had to make up my mind whether or not I should divulge a confidence and tell you who killed Posfort."

"I see." He leaned forward. "And who did kill him?"

"My father-in-law," Haze told him quietly.

The room had a deadly quiet. The tick of the clock was suddenly like the beat of a hammer on anvil.

"I see," Wharton said. "You're prepared to make a statement to that effect?"

"Yes, but only provided it's not made public. I won't stand for any smearing of a dead man's name."

"But what you've just told us has already smeared his name."

"Oh no," Haze said quickly. "I regarded it as a kind of . . . well, like being at a confessional."

"Very well," Wharton said. "Let's keep it like that—for the moment. You're prepared to tell us about it, purely confiden-tially?"

"Why not? The trouble is, it doesn't amount to a great deal. It was about a week after the actual murder, and he came up to Town and had lunch with us. Just an ordinary service lunch with a glass of port after it, and then my wife had to go and he and I sat on talking. We'd both thought he was looking shockingly ill and I asked him how he really was, and that sort of thing. It was pretty difficult, because I didn't want to get him on the subject of Caroline. Then he suddenly told me point-blank that he'd killed Posfort. It caught me clean in the wind. I was absolutely speechless. I tried to laugh it away, but he insisted."

He looked at Wharton and he had a side look at me. Neither of us said a word.

"I tried to get him to tell me how he'd done it; you know, trying to check up with what had been in the papers and catching him out over something. What I was beginning to think was that he'd read all about everything and had deluded himself into thinking he was the one. But he wouldn't tell me a thing. He just told me again that he was the one who'd killed Posfort, and then he said he had to be going. I was absolutely scared. He said he was going straight back to Ralehurst, but I thought he might be going to the police, so I got him a taxi and actually saw him on the train."

The room was heavy again with quiet. Wharton gave a little grunt.

"You believed him?"

"I did. I had every reason to. You see, I happened to know it was he who had taken that gun."

Wharton stared.

"You're sure about that?"

"Absolutely sure. It was like this. When James came home we had a lunch party at the flat. A kind of celebration. Just the family, and afterwards we were going to Bridget's matinée to round things off. She had to leave a bit early, and I and my father-in-law and James were in my room and I was showing James that gun. I told you about that. I put it back and we went out, but when I looked round for the rector he hadn't come and then he did come, if you know what I mean. Then that very evening I happened to go to that drawer and the gun wasn't there, or the bullets—except the four or five you saw. James hadn't been in that room again, so there you are."

He shrugged his shoulders.

"I didn't know what to think. The whole thing was so damn silly. What should *he* want a gun for?"

"What'd he say when you asked him?"

Haze looked surprised.

"Who told you I asked him?"

"A logical question," Wharton said airily.

"Well, I did ask him. Not directly. 'You didn't happen to see that gun?' That sort of thing. He looked absolutely bewildered. I didn't like pestering him. That was the time when he was beginning to act a bit queer."

"You spoke to his son?"

"Directly—no. I'd already told him most earnestly to let me know of any deterioration in his father's health, and I thought that would include anything queer he might say, like having killed Posfort. And that was why I got him away to that private nursing home. The doctor's a friend, and I warned him he might say some most unusual things and it would be as well not to pay any attention to them."

"I see. And you said nothing to your wife?"

"My wife?" He stared. "You can't be serious. Tell her her father had owned up to killing Posfort!" He gave a little snort of annoyance. "And why do you think I insisted on all this being confidential? What good would it do her reputation if it ever got out?"

"Yes," Wharton said. "I see your point. And that's all you can tell us?"

"Absolutely all."

"Anything you'd like to ask, Mr. Travers?"

"Only one thing," I said. "Did your father-in-law have a car? I didn't see one when I was down there the second time."

"For a very good reason," he said. "He had an old Vauxhall, but James messed it up pretty badly. It was in dry dock."

"When did this messing-up take place?"

"Let me think," he said. "It was just after you came down that first time. He'll tell you if you ring him."

"An accident, was it?"

"Yes, and not altogether his fault. A stationary car round a corner and an oncoming car and no time to pull up. He said he was lucky to get off without a scratch."

There were no more questions. Haze asked about a statement.

"At the moment it wouldn't be worth the paper it's written on," Wharton told him calmly.

Haze bridled up.

"Are you trying to tell me you doubt my word?"

"Just the opposite," Wharton said suavely. "You know the old tag—'What the soldier said isn't evidence'. What you've said isn't evidence. It will be if we can get it in any way supported."

"Who's to support it?"

"You never know. He blurted something out to you and he might have done the same to someone else: the cook or the maid or the doctor or someone at that nursing home."

"Yes," Haze said slowly. "I hadn't thought about that."

Five minutes later Haze had gone and Wharton was wanting to know what I'd thought of it all. I said that Haze had spoken convincingly. I added that that was nothing to go by. Acting was his business.

"I know," he said. "Far as I'm concerned, though, I just can't believe it. Mind you, I can believe Halsing killed Posfort. Or could have killed him. He had reason to, according to that eye for an eye business he was maundering about when he was here that day. And I'd say he had the brains to plan it. Yet I'm damned if I believe he did it."

"If he did, then everything we've arrived at is wrong," I said. "We know the Posfort Case and the Alton Case are one and the same thing. Scrap that, and we're back where we started weeks ago."

"You think I don't know that? Why should old Halsing use Alton for an alibi? How could Halsing have induced him to go to Ralehurst? Halsing didn't know Alton existed. There's no possible connection between the two—except that Haze is Halsing's son-in-law. Something's badly wrong. The trouble is I can't put my finger on it. Unless—"

That sneer of a smile was directed at me. I was supposed to ask the question.

"Unless what, George?"

"Unless the whole thing's bunkum. Halsing's dead, isn't he? A nice convenient confession and we can't ask him about it—not this side of eternity. Very handy for Haze, if he did the job himself."

"Yes," I said. "And if so, what're you going to do about it?"

"Only one thing—keep working away on Haze. All the same, the Big Bugs'll have to hear all about what's happened this afternoon."

He didn't say when the pow-wow would be. It was getting on for six o'clock and I said I'd be going. He actually thanked me—not so surprising, perhaps, since I'd been working for nothing—and said he might be giving me a ring later.

I went home to an early dinner, to compensate for a missed tea. Wharton didn't ring, and at the usual time I went to bed. I'd done some thinking that evening and all that had emerged from it was the conviction that it was the Alton Case that held the vital clues. When I woke in the morning it was with just one small part of that case on my mind.

Don't ask me why it was that one queer offshoot was making the cloud on my mind. That subconscious process of selection works in its own way. It's what makes a hunch, though even hunches are more often wrong than right. What I woke with that morning was that same feeling I had had when Wharton and I had left behind us the factory of Vargo Products Limited: the feeling that there was something wrong about Tweed. I had expected a man who would be, and act like, an important executive: not necessarily a man of culture but at least a man who had about him some aura of big business, an authority, a confidence and a certain suavity. But Tweed, by those standards, had been almost an impostor. All he had had was a cheap boastfulness and a servility.

I couldn't pin it down to more than that, but something was telling me I might do worse than pay him another visit. I had been there with Wharton and that would give the entrée. What

I should be looking for I didn't know. But that didn't worry me. Ideas would come: at least they usually had.

17

THE WOOD AND THE TREES

IT WAS half-past ten when I arrived at the factory, and by daylight I saw it was a bigger place than I'd imagined. Not only did buildings run away to the left, but when I took a look at the back there were more buildings there. And there was plenty of activity. Lorries were coming in and vans were loading up, and from the back especially there was the steady hum and whirr of machinery. In a large parking place were about a dozen cars.

I went up the steps and into the main entrance. Just inside the doors was something I'd missed before—the word ENQUIRIES, with an arrow pointing down. I went through the door and was at a kind of counter like that of a post-office. Over one of the grilles was GENERAL ENQUIRIES. I asked the man behind it if I could see Mr. Tweed. I gave my own name, and waited while he rang.

"Sorry, sir," he said, "but Mr. Tweed is in conference. He won't be free for a time. Can I take a message?"

I'd been hoping to get information about Tweed without having to see him, but there were other people getting information in that room and it certainly wasn't a place for gossip.

"Could I see his secretary, Miss Cherry?"

He rang again. Miss Cherry would see me. I said I knew the way up.

I tapped at the door of Tweed's office and went in. Nobody was there. Maybe, I thought, I should have tapped at the last door I'd passed. But there was a door through to the right of Tweed's desk, and I was about to go towards it when my eye caught that sales chart. I had a look at it. The red line, as I had guessed, represented advertising costs. Then I had a look at one of those framed photographs. Underneath it was:

ADVERTISING STAFF—1953
(Vargo Products Limited)

The staff seemed uncommonly large, though the photograph was pretty compact. About twelve girls—typists probably—were standing on something, probably forms, at the back; another twelve were standing in front of them and seated in front were about another dozen people, most of them men. Tweed was easy enough to spot. He was sitting almost in the centre.

There was a sound and I whipped round. A woman was coming through the door beyond Tweed's desk. She was thin, alert-looking and in the thirties.

"Miss Cherry? My name's Travers. I was here an evening or two ago seeing Mr. Tweed. I was hoping to see him again this morning."

She told me what I already knew. Her manner was pleasant enough, but her voice was a bit aggressive.

"Perhaps I can handle whatever it is myself," she said.

"That's good of you, but I'm afraid not. It was rather a personal matter."

She definitely pricked her ears at that. I thought I might as well explore.

"You've been here a long while, Miss Cherry?"

"Ever since I was sixteen."

"Working with Mr. Tweed?"

"Oh no," she said, and the tone had a curious deprecation. "I've only been working with him for the last few weeks."

"Then you haven't always been in this department?" She looked a bit surprised.

"Not always. About six years."

I must have looked puzzled.

"But I thought Mr. Tweed had been in charge here all the time."

"Him?" she said with a sniff. "He was in the export department, and then he came here about eighteen months ago when that new advertisement was started. I suppose it was his idea. Mr. Haze had him brought here."

"Haze?"

"Yes," she said. "He's one of the directors and he was in charge here. He's only left a few weeks. Switched over to Productions, and that's why Mr. Tweed took over."

I gave her a nice smile.

"And, strictly between ourselves, you preferred working for Mr. Haze?"

"Yes," she said bluntly. "Mr. Haze was a gentleman. And considerate."

I thanked her and said I'd be going. Perhaps she'd be so good as to tell Mr. Tweed I'd called.

"By the way, I was looking at this photograph. You seem to have quite a big staff. This is you, isn't it?"

"Yes," she said. "Everyone says it's very good of me."

"And who's this between you and Mr. Tweed? His face seems familiar."

"That's Mr. Haze." Her finger began pointing. "That's the head photographer and that's Mr. Ames, his assistant. That's . . ."

I let her finish.

"Well, it's a very nice group. But about Mr. Haze. Now I come to think of it I met him once somewhere. This surely can't be he. Far as I remember he had a moustache."

She laughed.

"Oh, he only began growing that a short time ago. You must have seen him since."

"Maybe you're right," I said. "Or it might have been someone else."

I held out my hand.

"Goodbye, Miss Cherry. Give Mr. Tweed my message. And mention me to Mr. Haze if you see him."

She came the few steps to the door. She cleared her throat with a little cough.

"Excuse me, but weren't you one of the two gentlemen who were asking about photographs the other evening?"

"Yes," I said. "But it was something quite different I wanted to see Mr. Tweed about this morning."

I gave her another quick smile and moved on to the lift. I knew she must have been intrigued, as well as annoyed, by that hunting through photograph files, and probably she'd made inquiries from the girl who'd taken Wharton and me to Tweed's room. But that was only a passing thought. It was something far more important that was beginning to hammer away at me. I wasn't even gratified at that solving of the mystery of Tweed— the man who'd suddenly been put in charge of the whole department and who couldn't conceal a complacency, or even perhaps a jealousy. Those photographs had been his idea and yet he had had to work under Haze. Now he was the boss, and he wasn't minding who knew it.

But that was unimportant, as I said. What mattered was that till about the time of the Posfort murder Roland Haze had been in charge of advertising. He—like Tweed at the moment—had handled personally all competition photographs that had come in. He alone knew *what* photographs. He could have seen a photograph of his brother, and pocketed it, and handed the rest to Tweed or Miss Cherry for action or filing. That was why there was no photograph of Courtney Haze in the files.

I was still in my car, thinking things out. Roland, I told myself, might have shown that photograph to his brother as a kind of joke or leg-pulling. But his brother had retained it and the name and address. Courtney Haze had, in fact, killed Posfort. What he had told Wharton and me about his dead father-in-law had been merely a covering-up for himself.

My hand went to the gear lever and then drew back. I got out of the car and went up the steps again and to the lift. I tapped at the door just before Tweed's. A girl opened it and looked at me enquiringly against the sound of typewriters.

"Ask Miss Cherry to see me, will you?"

"Miss Cherry?" She gave a smile and turned back, the door just ajar. Almost at once Miss Cherry was coming out to the corridor.

"So sorry to bother you again," I said, "but I just remembered that I did know your Mr. Haze. Do you think I might see him?"

"Oh no," she said. "He's at that conference. All the heads of departments are."

"A pity," I said, "but I might see him later." The smile was a bit sheepish. "Funny I didn't recognise him. It was that moustache of his. How long did you say he'd grown it?"

"Let me see," she said. "He went to Productions at the end of October." She smiled. "That's when he began growing a moustache. I met him about a fortnight afterwards and, do you know, I didn't recognise him at first. Silly of me, wasn't it? And, of course, his glasses. He'd only just had to wear glasses."

"Well, tell him I called," I said. Another goodbye smile and I was making for the lift. I went out to the car and drove quietly away from Vargo Products Limited. About a quarter of a mile down the road was a police-station, and I drew the car in. The station sergeant didn't know me, but he let me use the telephone. Wharton, I was told, was in conference.

"I've got to speak to him," I said. "It's a matter of extreme urgency. You've got to get him on the line."

"It's most unusual, sir. You ought to know that."

"That's why I'm ringing."

"Very well, sir," I was told resignedly, and after that I had to wait. It must have been five minutes before I heard the indignant voice.

"Listen to me," I said. "I'm ringing from near Vargo's factory. I've just made a couple of really vital discoveries and I want to make a couple more—"

"What discoveries?"

"Unofficial ones. The next two have to be official and I'd like your authority."

"What are they? Seems to me you'd better get along here."

"There's no time," I said. "It's Christmas Eve and we've got to work fast. You tell me to go ahead and I'll be with you at two o'clock at the latest."

There was a moment's silence, then he was asking if I realised the position I was putting him in.

"If I didn't, I shouldn't be ringing you," I said. "You give me the word to go ahead and I think I can promise we'll have everything cleared up by tonight."

"You only think?"

"Some of us are only human," I told him. "Do I go ahead or don't I?"

"All right," he said. "But be here at two o'clock. And what you say had better be good."

I drove to the Royalty Hotel and saw Warren, the manager. He saw no reason why I shouldn't have a word with Ellen Lumley, if she was on duty. She was, and he went with me upstairs. We found her cleaning a room on the heels of a departed guest. She remembered me well enough, and that November evening. Probably she'd never forget it.

Warren left us. I told Ellen I'd like to go over once again what had happened on that November night. I'd sit on the bed to bring my head below hers and she must imagine me lying on the floor. I was the dying man and I wanted her to listen to what I had to say.

Five minutes later I had given her a tip and was back in Warren's office. I got a Marland number and rang it. The one I wanted was in. It took a little time, but I got the information I wanted. I thanked Warren, told him to keep things strictly to himself, and went out to the car again. This time I had to drive to the heart of the city. The streets were cluttered with eve-of-holiday traffic and it was half-past twelve when I got to Savenhall Street. The man I wanted was out to lunch. I got the name of a couple of likely places and found him in the first—a pub with a lunch service. The place was packed, and when I spotted him from the description I'd been given I saw he was sharing a table with three other men. Their main course had only just come, so I went back to the snack bar and had a beer and some sandwiches.

I thought my man was never coming out. His meal was over, but there was talk going on over coffee. It was after half-past one when he made a move. I buttonholed him as he came out. I had had no time to collect my warrant card, but I induced him to believe me. In ten minutes or so I had what I needed and by then we were at the place where I had parked the car. I told him to ring the Yard and check up on me when he got back to his office, but he must have taken me at my face value, for he never rang. I moved the car on. It was about two minutes past two when I went into Wharton's room, and I felt as if I'd been running in a marathon.

I hadn't time to hang up my overcoat before Wharton was wanting to know what it was all about. Matthews was there. So was the Commander, Crime—and he couldn't have dropped in just by chance. He gave me a nod and a smile.

"You look pleased with yourself," he told me.

I said he'd misinterpreted my look. My smile had been rueful.

"Everyone assembled," I said. "Ready to jump with six pairs of feet if I've slipped up."

"Next time we'll hang out the flags," he told me. "But have you slipped up?"

"That'll be for you to judge," I said. "I'm not dead certain, if that's what you mean. One thing ought to be done, though. I'll try and justify it in a minute or two. A couple of men ought to be rushed to the Vargo factory to pick up Roland Haze when he leaves. It's Christmas Eve and he might be going early. Later this evening we might have to know just where he is."

"Let me get this straight," Wharton said. "Are you telling us that Roland Haze is our man?"

"Yes," I said. "At least I'm practically sure."

"What's the evidence?"

"Only the old hashed up. And his brother."

"Just a minute," the C.C. said. "You're suggesting collusion?"

"No," I said. "But Courtney Haze tried to induce us yesterday to believe that he'd had to get away by himself for half an hour in order to think whether he'd be justified in telling us his father-in-law had committed the Posfort murder. You'll probably have gone into that, but what I think now is that he wanted that half-hour for something quite different—for ringing up his brother and trying to get the truth, and warning him."

Wharton gave Matthews a nod. Matthews went out. "What put Courtney Haze on to his brother?"

"That's where we begin guessing," I said. "The likelihood that he knew his brother had taken the gun. The knowledge that, as he didn't use Alton's photograph himself, his brother must have used it. Other things, perhaps, that may come out."

"And that's all you've got?" Wharton asked me.

"Not at all. I haven't really begun."

The C.C. got to his feet.

"Let's get along to my room. We'd better have everything taken down while you talk."

At a quarter to five that afternoon the last message came through from Marland. One man was ringing from the local police-station while the other watched the house. Haze had just arrived home.

"Right," Matthews said. "Get back to the house and keep it watched. If he attempts to leave, hold him."

A minute or two later we were off. Matthews sat with the driver and Wharton and I in the rear. It was as unlike a Christmas Eve as any I'd known; another muggy night with an overcast sky.

"You think he'll have tried to bolt?" Wharton asked me.

We tossed the question to and fro, if only to pass the time. Roland Haze in any case would have been in for a dull Christmas: old Halsing's death had settled that. No festivities at Quinton Place or Ralehurst, and therefore a Christmas at Marland. On the other hand he had every reason, or so we hoped, for wanting to bolt. His brother had warned him, Miss Cherry must have reported my morning visit, since I'd explicitly asked her. Tweed would have been questioned. If all that didn't show the writing on the wall, then Roland Haze was either an innocent man or remarkably slow in the upstake.

"If he does manage to bolt, he'll make for Spain," Wharton said. "A fat lot of chance he'll have too. I'm betting he'll be home when we get there, and that he'll try and bluff it all out."

*

We made faster time when we were off the main road. We came into the village by the bungalow end and went round the small green and towards the station. The car drew up twenty yards short of the cottage. The three of us got quietly out and stood for a minute till our eyes were used to the dark. A man came towards us on the grass verge and we could see him ten yards away.

"He's still in, sir. A light in the kitchen, but none in the front."

"You're sure it isn't his woman who's in the kitchen?" Matthews was asking.

"No, sir. She left a few minutes ago."

"Right," he said. "One of you at the back and one at the front."

The man moved off.

Wharton took Matthews by the arm.

"Don't forget what I told you. We're risking no more of this suicide business. Any time he looks like slipping anything into his mouth, collar him. You're responsible, so let's get going."

We moved off along the road. Beyond its hedge the cottage stood as a nearer blackness against the impalpable dark of the sky. Matthews slipped ahead and opened the front gate. Our feet seemed to clatter like hooves as we moved along the paved path. Wharton went into the lead. He listened at the door, then pushed the bell. We could hear the sound of it in the house.

There was no answering sound. Wharton gave a grunt, listened again, and his fingers went from the white surround of the bell to the dark of the knocker. The noise echoed as if in an empty house.

"What the devil's happened! Think we shall have to break in?"

He grasped the door handle and leaned as if to put his weight against the door. He went forward and for a moment I thought he'd fallen. The door had been unlocked. Ahead, along the short passage, light came from under the door—the kitchen door. Wharton felt for the light switch. He motioned us in and quietly closed the front door. He opened the door on his right, switched on the light and looked in. He switched the light off and looked in the room on his left. He switched that light off. The light in the passage stayed on.

"Watch the stairs," he whispered to Matthews, and went gently along to the kitchen door. Beyond it I could hear a faint sound. Wharton tried the handle. The door didn't move.

"Who's there?"

That was Haze's voice: not a scared voice, not even a surprised one. A queer kind of voice that I couldn't quite place.

"Superintendent Wharton of New Scotland Yard. I'd like a few words with you, Mr. Haze."

"Just a moment," he said, and almost at once we heard the drawing back of a bolt and then the door opened.

"Just been having my meal," he said, and he was wiping his lips with his napkin. His eyes went from Wharton to me, and I could have sworn he smiled.

"You say you want a word with me?"

"If you please, sir—yes. Several words."

Matthews moved forward and into the kitchen. Haze laid the napkin on the table.

"Then we'd better go into the lounge. It's more comfortable there."

"After you, then, sir."

"Thank you," Haze said, and smiled. He moved along the passage, and suddenly I was feeling tremendously uneasy. About Haze there was nothing of fright or even perturbation. His manner was as quiet and mild and as shyly courteous as it had always been: it wasn't the manner of a guilty man.

But he was halting at the door and waving for Wharton to go in.

"After you, sir."

"Thank you," Haze said, and went in. "Do sit down and make yourselves comfortable. There's a fire, as you see. In fact, I was expecting you to call."

18

THE LAST WORD

HAZE had drawn his chair somewhat away from the fire so as to face us. Matthews stood slightly behind him, leaning against the wall. Wharton had the chair opposite. I sat in a corner of the small chesterfield and I could have touched Haze if I'd just reached out a hand.

"You know why we've come, then," Wharton had said as we were sitting down.

"I'm not sure," Haze told him slowly. "I had an idea someone might want to ask me some questions."

Matthews leaned over. Haze was only taking a pipe from his pocket.

"Do smoke if you want to," he told us, and began filling the pipe from his pouch.

"You'd like to tell us why you thought we'd have questions to ask?" Wharton said.

Haze's pipe was going. He leaned slightly back in the chair, an elbow on its arm.

"I'm sorry, but I can't tell you that. I just knew it."

"Very well. Well ask a few questions. You begin, Mr. Travers."

Most of what I'd rehearsed had already gone. Haze's attitude was still worrying me. There was an indifference about him. He wasn't a man who was suddenly on trial for his life.

"We'd like to question you about killing Posfort," I said. "We know that either you or your brother killed him. We had ideas about that before, but the alibis held us up. Now we have a witness who can prove it. Posfort didn't die at once. He lingered a few minutes, and this witness of ours heard his last words. You can guess what they were?"

He was looking puzzled.

"I'll tell you. He managed to say this: *Haze shot me. Haze—* Then he died. Only two Hazes, you can't dispute that. Either you shot Posfort or your brother did. We're suggesting that you did. The fact that you'd no apparent connection with the man Alton tied us up too. Now we know that you're the very image of your brother and that's why you grew that moustache. Things that are equal to the same thing are equal to one another. Alton's photograph was like your brother and therefore like you."

"I see." He suddenly looked up. "About what Posfort said. It isn't some sort of trap?"

"We don't lay traps," Wharton told him curtly. "We're telling the truth. Posfort wouldn't have lied either. He knew you and he knew you'd shot him."

"Yes," Haze said, and as if to himself. "If that's so, then I must admit I shot him."

"You realise what you're saying? It's my duty to warn you."

"There's no need," he said. "I shot him. I shot him for what he did to Caroline. Caroline Halsing."

He leaned forward and he might have been talking about Spain or his garden or the weather.

"I had a letter. Everyone knew she wrote two letters, but they didn't know that one was for me. She said that when I got it she'd be dead. And she told me why. And she said she knew the mistake she'd made and how it was me that she—that she should have married." The lip drooped as he looked at us, almost shyly. "You don't think me much, perhaps, for anyone like Caroline, but we'd have been happy. I may choose to live here quietly, but I'm not a poor man. I could have given her everything if it hadn't been for Posfort."

"But Alton," I said. "He didn't kill Caroline Halsing."

He winced as he looked away. His voice was suddenly very tired.

"It had to be done. There wasn't any other way. I didn't really want to kill him. I didn't even watch him die. I came back afterwards and I turned off the light and got him to the kitchen. There's a door there to the garage."

"He'd accepted you as your brother?"

His eyes were blinking.

"Sorry," he said. "I'm a bit tired. It's been a tiring day."

"Did Alton take you for your brother?" I asked him again.

"Yes," he said. "I told him I was growing the moustache for a new film. I said I wanted him for a special kind of understudy, but I had to try him out. He put on a moustache and wore my old British warm and my hat and went to that concert for me."

"And Rickson saw something wrong. So he had to be killed."

He laid the pipe carefully down.

"I didn't mean to kill anyone. Only Posfort. Then I seemed to be in a sort of trap. . . ."

The tired voice trailed away. He leaned back in the chair, eyes closed.

"Rickson asked you about it on the train the next morning. He spoke to Alton and Alton shied away. He mentioned it to Lord and Lord later on mentioned it to you, and you said anyone would want to shy away from Rickson. Lord thought it a very good answer. That was lucky for Lord or you might have killed him too."

Haze lay back with eyes closed. He might have heard never a word.

"What about that Berlin letter?" Wharton asked him. "You were in Paris on your way to Spain just before it was sent. Who posted it for you? Some Frenchman?"

Haze's head went forward. Matthews held him or he would have fallen from the chair. Wharton shot across.

"What's the matter with him?"

"Don't know, sir, but he's not right."

"Get some water or something."

Matthews went out to the kitchen. I lent Wharton a hand and we got Haze to the chesterfield. The body was absolutely limp and the breathing stertorous. Wharton was staring.

"What is it? A fit?"

He drew back the eyelid. He shook his head.

"Might be something he took. Can't see much wrong with the eyes. Colour's a bit blue."

He looked up as Matthews came in.

"Where's the water?"

"Didn't know if we'd want it," Matthews told him, and gave him a little cardboard tube. "This was on the side of the sink."

"My God!" Wharton said. "It's Cenophine!"

"Yes," Matthews said. "That Caroline Halsing killed herself with an overdose of Cenophine."

There had been a minute or two of something like panic, then Matthews had gone to find the whereabouts of the nearest doctor. Wharton had come back to say Matthews had taken the car to fetch him from the next village. It'd be quicker that way.

"How's the pulse?"

"Not so good," I said. "Much weaker than it was."

Wharton fussed round impatiently, then went into the passage to do some telephoning. I could hear his voice droning on as I stood in that quiet room, looking down at Haze.

Somehow I couldn't think of him as a murderer, but then, as I've said, I was never really cut out for a detective—the hard-boiled type that sees only a crime and a criminal. Haze to me was still a man I had known. And I knew how right about him I had been, and how wrong.

That love of his for Caroline Halsing hadn't been the aberration I had thought it, but the one great thing in his life. Once he had been certain that she thought him merely a kind of elder brother, then he had been content to be only in the background of her life. I had liked him. Somehow, and in spite of everything, I still liked him, and the pity that suddenly flooded me had in it a sense of loss.

It was that letter of hers that had changed him. What had been pent up had been released and had taken possession. His life from that moment had been the knowledge that he had a duty—to kill Posfort. Was it a kind of madness? I supposed it was. A schizophrenia—yes. From the moment of that resolve he had been two men: one who could plan to the last detail a cold-blooded, remorseless murder, and the other a man who could still wince with the repugnance at what that one killing had also meant. Alton and Rickson. He had been so sickened at the death of one that he hadn't been able to watch him after that fatal drink, and the other man had been struck down in the dark.

There was the sound of the car. Voices, steps on the path and the door opening. I heard Wharton say something, and then Matthews came in. An elderly man was with him, carrying the usual bag.

"The doctor," Matthews told me.

Wharton was coming in. The doctor was bending over Haze. I moved out of the way towards the door. The doctor straightened himself.

"Too late," he said. "He's gone."

Wharton grunted.

"Anything we should have done?"

"Don't think so," the doctor said. "May I have a look at that container?"

"Cenophine, all right," he said. "A proprietary name. Made up in twenties. He probably took the whole lot. Might have taken something else to make sure. Can't tell till we've explored. You'd still like to get him away?"

I moved into the passage. Another car drew up, probably the ambulance. I went on to the kitchen. The light was on as Matthews had left it. On the table was a cold meal, and it looked untouched. A light in the kitchen when we'd arrived, but none in the lounge. Haze must have been watching from the lounge window and had seen our man keeping an eye on the house. Everything had been ready in the kitchen, and as soon as we'd arrived he'd taken those tablets. It was the water that he'd been wiping from his mouth with the napkin when we'd opened the door.

I noticed that door that opened into the garage and I thought about Alton and how Haze must have questioned him and been sure that Alton had said nothing to a single soul. His own lie had killed Alton. Maybe if he had mentioned that cryptic letter to Joan Crewe he'd have been still alive, and Posfort would have been alive too. Or would Haze have killed him in some other way?

I heard voices and I looked out to the passage. Haze's body was being taken out, and I turned back. A minute or two and I heard the ambulance drive off. Wharton came back, and I joined him in the empty lounge.

"Well, that's that," he said. "No use blaming us for what happened. One of those things you couldn't foresee."

He gave a grunt or two.

"Who'd have thought it? An inoffensive chap like that. You wouldn't have thought he could hurt a fly. But I told you, didn't

I? Crippen was an inoffensive chap too. I told you this Haze was the man for my money."

"Yes," I said. "And what do we do now? Get back to the Yard?"

"Nothing else for us here," he said. "Matthews will have a look round. I'd like to find that letter he said that Caroline girl wrote him—just to help round things off. It ought to be about somewhere. It wasn't in his pockets."

"Might as well be going, then," I said. "It's feeling a bit chilly in here now."

"Feels stuffy to me," he said. "But about that gun. Wasn't there something fishy about that crazy-paving he was doing? In the morning I'll have it up. Wouldn't mind betting we find the gun under it. And whatever it was he killed Rickson with."

"You're probably right," I told him. "I hadn't thought of that."

"I don't know," he said as he closed the front door, "but you haven't done so bad yourself. In fact I don't know when you've ever done better."

I followed him down the path and I was wondering; not about that but how long it would take me to forget the face of Roland Haze. The car was drawing up at the gate and Matthews was asking Wharton something about his men. I stood by the car, waiting. Below us a train was pulling out of the station, and in that damp evening air the sound was uncannily close. Then back towards the village there was the tentative sound of church bells. They changed to a sudden rhythm, and it was then that I remembered again that it was Christmas Eve.

THE END

Lightning Source UK Ltd.
Milton Keynes UK
UKHW010147231121
394397UK00001B/33

9 781913 527136